ECOLUTION

ERIK STEVENSON

Lazy Dog Press
Fort Collins, CO

To my wife
I am grateful for everything,
particularly your inspiration

CONTENTS

Dwindling Reserves

Kendra slammed the window shut.

"Why do I ever open windows? This house is drafty enough without me being a dumbass. I might as well throw money out it," she said. She loved the feeling of cold crisp air coming in the house, especially in the spring, and often sat near an open window breathing it in. Her husband Nikolaj sat on their tattered couch looking up at her with a concerned look.

Barely a thousand square feet, the 1950's home sat on a skinny lot surrounded by other homes of the same vintage. The difference, however—the *big* difference—between their quaint house and the rest was that their home hadn't been updated since the eighties. They knew this based on the newest items being hideous gold-plated, beveled glass light fixtures. She was certain that the insulation and windows were all original. Original, not in the good sense of the word.

The surrounding million-dollar homes were all updated inside and out. Don, the single, retired bachelor next door, had invited them over for dinner a few weeks after they moved in. Nikolaj later told Kendra that he never would have guessed that Don's house was built in 1952. It was a gorgeous home that could easily have been featured in Architectural Digest. Kendra thought it just might have been. From the immaculate nature of Bill and Judy's home from the outside, Kendra figured their home was much the same. Though they would never know. In a tremendously awkward conversation one day, Judy told Kendra that they didn't let people in their house because they didn't want to bring in diseases that might kill their cats. *Wow,* thought Kendra.

Kendra and Nikolaj's home, having not been updated, was half the value. They had been lucky to find it. Downtown Boulder home prices had skyrocketed over the last few years. Though their home was substantially cheaper, they still had to stretch to afford it.

"You enjoy the fresh air, babe. Don't be so hard on yourself."

There were bills strewn about on the floor and a Moleskin notebook open showing their budget for the year—all around a circle on the living room floor where Kendra had just been sitting. She stared down at the bills. Their dog, Coda, looked down from his perch on the couch in nearly the same glassy eyed manner.

"We don't have enough in our account to pay the mortgage. I had to throw in another thousand earlier this month to cover business expenses," she said.

Nikolaj puffed out his cheeks and sighed. "No problem, let's take another two-thousand out of my retirement account—we can do that without paying a penalty."

"I can't keep doing that to you."

"It's *our* money and this is an investment. We moved down here so you could start your business. We knew it would be hard, but you're so close to making it all work. As soon as you get the work approved for the enhancements they want along with the support contract you already have, you're golden."

"What happens if we don't get it? What happens if some other unexpected expense comes through? We're done. We're all tapped out and would have to rely solely on Jacqui. She's done a better job of saving but probably doesn't have more than six months' worth of business expenses saved. She's already put almost her entire life savings and retirement in. If this doesn't work out, she'll have to start from scratch."

Tears were starting to well up in her eyes. She turned and walked toward the kitchen, opening the cabinet to get a glass for water she didn't need. Kendra didn't need Nikolaj to see her cry again.

"If this doesn't work, we'll have to start from scratch again, too," she said.

"It'll work."

She spun back around, nearly breaking the glass against the side of the counter. "How do you know? One thing, that's all it's going to take. One thing, and we're done. Nikolaj, I love the support and optimism, but we've got to be realistic. This could all go south pretty easily."

Nikolaj stood up and walked over to the half wall between the kitchen and living room. He put his elbows on the wall and head in his hands, running his hands through is long mane of hair.

"There's still fifty thousand in my retirement account. We'd have to start paying a tax penalty if we touch it, but it's there. We could sell the house. That'd be easy in this market. And we always have my job—that's pretty solid."

"I can't keep taking from *your* retirement."

"You keep saying that, but it's ours—we're in this together."

"And, your job. I know you think it's solid, but the majority of your funding is government money. The way things are going, that could be ripped right out from under your feet."

"We'll make it Kendra—I don't know how—but we'll figure something out."

Evolve

Kendra woke up to the sound of water lapping up against the side of a boat. It was her quiet alarm which was supposed to wake her gently only if she wasn't in a REM phase—it always woke her up. She thought about fixing that by lowering the volume or something but didn't bother. She liked getting up during the first alarm anyway. It meant she woke early and had time to think before going into work. It was 6 am.

She saw the light on under the bathroom door and heard the shower running. She realized Nikolaj must have already finished his run and breakfast, before showering and driving an hour north of their home in Boulder to Fort Collins where he worked.

The cool spring air was gently blowing through the crack she left in the window and she could smell the crisp air. She was glad spring was here and summer just around the corner. It had been a long winter. For Nikolaj's sake she was glad he didn't have to commute through the ice and snow—assuming they didn't get another "shoulder" snowstorm like they did last year. She wasn't sure that was a legitimate term but had heard it from one of Nikolaj's colleagues on the Colorado State

University campus. It made sense, so she used it when she could.

After lying in bed enjoying the fresh smell of the cool air and early morning sounds for a few minutes, she slowly slid out from under the warm covers and put her bare feet on the cold wood floor. She grabbed her sweatshirt and headed out to the kitchen, the old floors creaking as she walked. Nikolaj had already made a carafe of coffee in the French press. After having gone through several different types of coffee makers through the years, they had finally settled on the cheapest, easiest method.

She poured herself a cup and settled down on the couch to space out, looking out the window, thinking about what she needed to do at work. Their eleven-year-old black lab, Coda, came strolling out of the bedroom, did a slow downward dog yoga pose, and sidled up next to her on the couch.

She heard Nikolaj moving around in their bedroom and a few minutes later he came out dressed and ready to go.

"Morning hon," he said.

"Morning. You off?"

"Yep. Cat and Anir were finishing up the last of hooking up our data into your new system. If everything worked out, we should have some results this morning!"

"Great. Give me a call after you've had a chance to look through the output. Since your team is the first to put Ecolution to the test, I'd like to make sure everything is working as expected."

"Will do. Alright, I'm off. Talk later," he said, giving her a peck on the cheek before heading out the door. Coda's eyes rolled up to watch him leave, but otherwise he didn't move an inch.

Ecolution was the software that Kendra's company, Evolve Inc., had written for the U.S. Department of Agriculture and U.S. Geological Survey. It was a joint venture between the two agencies to improve the efficiency of scientific data collection and analysis. Nikolaj worked for both Colorado State University and the USGS as an Ecologist. His research on ice shelf stability in Antarctica and how it relates to climate change was a perfect initial test of the new system.

As cofounder and CTO of Evolve, Kendra had a large stake in making Ecolution succeed. She had no doubt it would but there was still a lot of work ahead of them. The software development was largely complete. Now they had the work of training the scientific teams on how to integrate their data and models with Ecolution ahead of them. There was also the matter of training the USDA staff on how to support and administer the software in their environments, and inevitably the bug fixes and maintenance. In the least, this work would take them through the next year.

Next week would be the big kickoff meeting at the USDA's National Information Technology Center up in Fort Collins. All the executive sponsors from both agencies, as well as many of the science teams that were part of the early adopter program would be attending.

In the meantime, there was still plenty to accomplish. These were the items running through Kendra's mind for the moment. Not that their office was stressful, but the few minutes she had in the morning before she got in were her few minutes alone to think. Once she got in, there wouldn't be much of that kind of time available.

She finished her coffee with a deep sigh and slowly stood up to start her day. After a quick shower she ate her usual oatmeal and banana, and popped her array of vitamins she took that good old Perlmutter and Colman recommended in their The Better Brain Book. She saw the book at the Stanford Bookstore a few years ago when curiosity got the best of her and she snuck down to the textbook section in the basement. The books were ordered by class and there ended up being few sections she skipped. This one caught her eye and she later bought a copy when she got home.

Kendra pulled out a few favorite brain toys for Coda to work on while she was gone and filled up his food toy with his breakfast. It was this large, red beehive-looking container with a weight at the bottom, so it bobbed around a bit when you nudged the side of it—like one of those inflatable punching bags that were popular for young kids in the 70's and 80's. The container had a small hole in the side of it, just large enough for kibble to fall out of it at a certain angle. It kept Coda active long enough to satisfy him until Kendra returned later in the day.

She locked up the house and walked down the street toward Broadway where she took that north up to the walking mall on Pearl Street. As she passed Central Park she noticed the man sitting on the steps near the bandshell. He'd been there every morning for the past week. There was something odd about him, but she couldn't quite put a finger on it. It was like he was watching her without truly looking at her. *Jesus, Kendra, you are super paranoid*, she thought. *Probably just another dude who recently sold his startup and now has more time on his hands than he knows what to do with.*

The Evolve office was up on the second level overlooking the mall. She enjoyed the walks, particularly this early in the morning. It was still quiet, and she could continue her near-meditation before she got to the office.

Fifteen minutes later she arrived and strolled through the door ready for the day. As usual she was the first in. She knew her employees well and headed straight to the kitchen to start a pot of coffee. She didn't need a cup right away, but knew that's where most of her staff would directly head when they got in.

It was now a few minutes before seven. She checked her calendar to see what the day had in store for her and saw the following:

7:30 am   Innovation Initiatives

8:00 am   Stand-up
8:30 am   Call with Security Firm
9:30 am   Call with USDA/USGS
10:30 am Tech Writer Interview
11:30 am Lunch with Brenda
1:00 pm   One-on-one with Mike
1:30 pm   Meet with Jeff (HR)
2:00 pm   Reading/Training
2:30 pm   Tech Writer Interview Debrief
3:00 pm   Recruiter debrief

The rest of the day looked pleasant though. She was looking forward to her lunch with Brenda. Brenda was a friend she met at a session during the Boulder Startup Week a few years ago. She owned a successful co-working facility in town and it was fun to talk shop with her. Brenda was diligent about keeping up on the latest advances in workspace productivity and generally had a lot of good tips that Kendra could apply to her own office.

After spending a half hour triaging and replying to email, she spent another half hour working through her latest initiative to roll out software releases more often. It was going to take both a technical solution and a cultural shift to make it happen. She had the technical solution worked out, but still needed to work through the cultural part. She knew most of her staff would jump on it right away, but there were a few she would have to get more buy-in before it got full traction.

She finished writing up her thoughts on that initiative and then walked down the hall to where the team was performing their morning status meeting—stand-up they called it. And an apt name for it. It was intended to be a quick meeting to make sure everyone had what they needed to get their work done and see how their work was tracking to the schedule. By standing up during the meeting they ensured that it wouldn't run too long. Kendra only peeked her head in through the door to listen. She didn't want to interrupt unless help was needed. Nothing came up, so she continued back to her office and onto her next call.

Mike, the technical lead for the team, and Katie, their internal security expert, came in just as she was dialing into the conference call. It was a call with a cyber security firm who was running security penetration tests against the Ecolution software. This was the final readout call where they went through each vulnerability they found in detail to make sure the Evolve team understood its impact and what needed to be done to fix it. Kendra was pleasantly surprised to see there were very few vulnerabilities identified. Though with Katie on the team, they had their own internal security expert who caught most potential vulnerabilities before they ever made it to the final software builds.

"Nice work both of you," Kendra said after she hung up the call. "This will make the end of the release much easier on everyone. We'll be able to focus on the final couple of bug fixes and testing before we make this available to all the teams."

"This was really all Katie," Mike replied, never having been good at handling a compliment. It was always his first instinct to share the praise, too, which had the added benefit of his team always having his back.

"Well, thanks Mike," said Katie, "but we all know you had a large hand in it as well. Take some credit for once and be happy with it. Anyway, enough of this love fest, I know you two have another meeting shortly with the customer. I'm going to see myself out and go do the important work of sitting behind my monitors with my headphones on, listening to some Korpiklaani and tuning the rest of the world out." She didn't bother waiting for a reply, knowing she left them with a conversation topic.

"Korpiklaani?" Kendra asked.

"What? You don't know the Finnish thrash metal band, Korpiklaani? Does Nikolaj not teach you anything about that area of the world?" Mike said sarcastically.

"Let's just say he has different tastes. Though he did have kind of a wild adolescence."

"Katie sent me a video of them once. I could hear her music coming out of her headphones and asked her what she was listening to—I could tell it was super intense. I just about died laughing when I watched it. It's this intense crazy. Have you ever listened to heavy metal—I mean *heavy* metal? Not Metallica heavy, but seriously heavy."

"A little."

"Well, this is seriously *heavy*—I think they call it thrash metal, actually. Anyway, it was a video of them in concert and the lead singer had like a deer skull on the front of his mic stand. I may have been laughing out of fright to be honest. But I guess it does the trick for Katie. She can sit there for hours listening to that stuff and churning out an amazing amount of code."

"Ha, I'm always amazed at what helps some of you focus. I'll stick to my classical music, thank you. Anyway, we should get over to Jacqui's office."

Jacqueline Phelps was the CEO and cofounder, along with Kendra. The two had met while they were both working at HP up in Fort Collins. Jacqui was a development manager for another team Kendra often worked with as an architect. Kendra was often working with other teams to either learn what they were doing and how or sharing what her team was doing. The two of them hit it off immediately and quickly became friends.

Ever since either of them had entered the software industry they had envisioned themselves starting their own company at some point. After getting to know each other, they realized they would be going into business together—it was just a matter of time and the right idea. It didn't take much time. Kendra always kept a fondness for science and was always looking for an opportunity to combine science with software engineering. Having married an ecologist, she spent a lot of her time talking about it, but that just wasn't enough.

At HP Kendra worked in the big data and analytics line of business. From having worked as an ecologist herself for the USGS to listening to Nikolaj talk about his work, she knew a lot of the scientific community kept in silos and didn't often share their data or resources—at least not on a grand scale. That's what gave them their initial idea—give the scientific community a way to pool their data.

As a manager, Jacqui knew there were going to be challenges with adoption. It didn't matter how brilliant the technical solution was. If the scientists were not motivated to pool their resources, they wouldn't buy it. Between Kendra's technical brilliance and Jacqui's business acumen, they knew they had something. So, two years prior, they both quit their jobs and began working on the initial vestiges of what would eventually become Ecolution.

With Nikolaj's contacts at the USGS where he had a position, Jacqui and Kendra began to pull together a plan and propose a solution that earned them a small contract. After delivering what now seems an insignificant prototype, their contacts at the USGS loved it and word quickly went up the chain to a Dr. Elizabeth Harrison, the Director of the Office of Science Quality and Integrity for the USGS. Dr. Harrison knew of the USDA's National Information Technology Center housed in the same building complex as the USGS offices in Fort Collins and thought expanding, what would become Ecolution, to both agencies, more science teams, and the scope of the software itself warranted a large contract. The large contract suddenly put Jacqui and Kendra on the hook to deliver something neither could do without the help of a highly qualified team of engineers. It wasn't that they weren't capable—they were plenty capable. But they would have needed to clone Kendra four times over to get the work done on time. After a lot of thought and debate, they settled on building their company and team in Boulder. Boulder's strong start-up environment and potential to pull strong engineers from Denver, Boulder, Fort Collins and areas in between, made it the ideal choice.

After two years of building a company, engineering team, and the product itself, they were getting ready to deliver it. Everyone on all sides saw the vast improvements Ecolution was going to bring and wanted to make sure it was going to succeed. This is what the meeting Kendra and Mike were heading into.

Kendra knocked on the door and peeked through the floor-to-ceiling window next to the door. Jacqui was talking to someone on the conference line and waved them in. Kendra opened the door and they both quietly walked in.

"Alright Bill, that sounds fair to me. We'll get you a proposal early next week. I gotta run to my next meeting, but will be in touch soon," Jacqui ended the meeting and hit the hang-up button.

"You two go ahead and dial in. I just need to fire off this email. How are you both doing?" said Jacqui.

"Good all around. Just wrapped up our call with Securial. I'll catch you up after this, but the short of it is we're in good shape. I'll talk through some of it on this call," Kendra replied as she was dialing into the conference call. The call went through and she entered the meeting code which she now knew by heart having dialed it so many times.

"Good morning, it's Kendra, Jacqui, and Mike from Evolve," Kendra said after the three beeps that told her she was in the call.

"Hi guys, it's just Gil so far. How are you all?" Gil Whittaker asked. Gil was the Deputy Associate Chief Information Officer in the Fort Collins USDA National Information Technology Center. Kendra had known him for a few years now and enjoyed a healthy, trusted working relationship.

"Doing well. How about you?" Kendra said.

"Can't complain. We'll give folks a few minutes and get started. Elizabeth just sent me a message saying she'd be a little late."

"Who are we expecting today?" Kendra asked.

"Elizabeth, Jack, Kerry, Anton, Randy, Maria, Richard, and Jim"

Kendra was already at Jacqui's whiteboard at the sound of Kerry's name. She knew Jacqui would know a few of those names, but not all, and wanted to make sure Jacqui could respond appropriately as people spoke on the call. They were quite the team. Mike had noticed a few times before how one would

16

answer a question before the other even began asking it. In a matter of twenty seconds she had two organization charts drawn up on the board—one for each agency—with names and titles. In the meantime, they heard several series of beeps as people joined the call and said their names.

"Ok, sounds like we're mostly all here with the exception of Jack," referring to Dr. Jack Denning, the Deputy Director of Research and Development for the U.S. Department of Agriculture. No one missed Jack, apart from Richard. Even that was debatable. "Let's go ahead and get started and Jack can join us when he's available. Jacqui, do you want to start off?" Gil asked.

"Actually, Gil, I'm going to wait until the end. I'll kick it over to Kendra to start off with our status," said Jacqui.

"Sure. Kendra, all yours," said Gil.

"Let's start with some fresh news then. Mike, Katie, and I just had our final readout call with Securial regarding the security audit. The test went well, and a few vulnerabilities were discovered but not many. We had two high impact, three medium, and six in the low to informational impact. We had already identified half of those and they are in the process of being fixed. If I know Mike at least a couple of them are likely already fixed," Kendra said as Mike shot her a sly grin.

"What were the two high impact vulnerabilities?" Richard interjected.

"The first was password storage in clear text in part of our log output; and the second was an unpadded cryptographic usage," said Kendra.

"I was aware of both of them before the tests started. We just didn't have the chance to fix them beforehand. They're fixed now," Mike added.

"And those will be in the next release before we head into further beta testing," said Kendra.

"So, you're saying we have clear text passwords being logged right now? Unbelievable!" Richard said.

"Likely not," said Mike. "That vulnerability is only applicable to the users and groups web service endpoints, and with your layers of security on top of that, like your firewall and strong operating system user passwords, you shouldn't be exposed."

"*Shouldn't*, that's not good enough. We should *never* be exposed!" said Richard.

"Jim, is our assumption that you aren't currently using those web services correct?" Kendra asked.

"Yes, that's correct," replied Jim.

"Thanks, Jim. If that is the case, you are not vulnerable," Kendra replied coolly.

"And what about the cryptography screw-up?" Richard shot back. Gil had little to no control over Richard and unless he was in a tight spot, didn't usually call Richard out when he was being disrespectful. He certainly didn't when Jack was on the line. Jack had told him before to back off on Richard, *he's only asking questions and providing some needed push-back on the vendor*. Unfortunately, Richard could waste hours of people's time going on about minutiae no one cared about. Jack did value his time enough to stop Richard when he was on the phone. Otherwise, Gil would let him ramble on with ten other people in the room, wasting all their time for hours.

Kendra and Jacqui, on the other hand, found it quite disruptive and counterproductive. Richard would not have lasted five minutes in the Evolve culture. They didn't mind team members questioning or challenging each other, if it was in a respectful way and the goal was to improve the team or the product.

"That vulnerability is also only used in the web services mentioned earlier—you are not currently exposed and will not be once you take our next release," Kendra answered.

"But we *could* be, is what you're saying," said Richard.

"I disabled those endpoints since we weren't using them," Jim said. You could always count on Jim to say very little, but just enough when it was required.

"As the security lead for the USDA, I need a list of the vulnerabilities identified," Richard said.

"The final document is already sitting in Gil's secure file transfer folder," Kendra said, immediately moving on. "We will be wrapping up this release for early next week. Mike and Peter will be onsite working with Jim on Tuesday morning. We are currently wrapping up this release, including fixes for the identified security vulnerabilities and the three bugs identified in the alpha release that were prioritized for this release."

"It sounds like things are coming together nicely, Kendra. Nice work. Gil, how many teams do we have slated to participate in the beta release?" said Elizabeth Harrison.

"Ten teams total from various parts of the country but all climate change related science," said Gil.

"And how are we collecting feedback regarding bugs, change requests, and new feature requests?" said Elizabeth.

"Joanne from Jim's team will be coordinating and handling those requests. We have an issue management system that is tied into Evolve's equivalent system, so they will see them as soon as Joanne gets them into our system. She'll be taking the information through the typical channels—phone, email, whatever people are comfortable with. But we're also trying another self-service method—a chatbot hooked up in the Ecolution Support chat room," said Gil.

"Do I even want to ask?" said Elizabeth.

"You do, it's pretty slick. And you can thank Mike for this," Gil began.

"I'd love to take the credit, but that was actually Peter from our team," Mike quickly jumped in. Kendra leaned over and whispered to Mike, "you know you *can* take credit for some things. I know you also worked on that and have the feeling you had a lot to do with the original idea." Mike blushed.

"Ah, alright—thank Peter. Whatever you do, don't thank Mike. Anyway, if you type in either, change request, feature request, or bug into the chatroom, a bot will ask you the relevant questions for that type of request and then log that information into the system for you once you're done," Gil finished.

"That's amazing—and a bit hysterical, with a dash of creepy. If I ever have to log anything, I will be picking up the phone and talking directly with Joanne. But I can see the attraction for some people," said Elizabeth.

"We'll go through it in more detail during the beta kickoff meeting, so everyone knows how to use it," said Gil.

"When is the kickoff meeting, Gil?" asked Kerry.

"That's on Wednesday of next week. It will be an all-day event hosted in the main conference room here in the Fort Collins office. We'll also have a conference line open with screen sharing and will record the meeting. So, if you can't travel or can't make it that day, you will still be able to see it one way or another," said Gil.

"And what's the agenda?" asked Kerry.

"The first half of the day will include Kendra and her team giving an introduction to the software, how to use it, how to create custom modules for data filtering for example. Then the second half of the day, Nikolaj Mikkelsen from the USGS, will be giving a demonstration of how his team used Ecolution during the alpha release phase and their experience.

And, Jim and his team will discuss support, and logging bugs and feature requests," said Gil.

"Great, thanks," said Kerry.

"Alright, we're a couple of minutes overtime and I've heard a couple of folks drop off already. Jacqui, I know you had something you wanted to discuss," said Gil.

"It can wait. I need to jump on my next call anyway," Jacqui answered.

"Is there anything else we need to cover?" said Gil. After a few seconds of silence, he continued. "Ok. Thanks everyone. Have a good rest of your day."

Jacqui hit the hang up button and sighed. "Nice job you two. Sounds like we're going into this next phase strong," she said.

"Thanks, Jacqui. Something not sitting quite right though. We need to keep our eye on Richard. Normally I'd say he's an unfortunate distraction, but there's something there I don't trust—something that's going to bite us if we're not careful. If I were Gil, that guy would have been gone a long time ago. But we don't have that luxury. Hopefully I'm making something out of nothing," said Kendra.

"I'm glad you mentioned that, Kendra. I get that sense too. Without Gil willing to stand Richard down, there may not be much we can do about it. We may have to mitigate that risk the best we can ourselves. Anyway, again good job. I need to dial into my next meeting so I gotta kick you two out," said Jacqui.

"Thanks," both Kendra and Mike said in unison as they headed out the door.

Kendra and Mike headed down the hall together toward the lobby. Kendra's next part of the day included interviewing a tech writer, who she hoped was already waiting for her. The previous interviewee showed up three hours late and the first thing out of his mouth was, "ah, jeez, I'm sorry but I completely spaced the interview." *Thanks, but no thanks*, she thought. *The next thing you will do is space out coming into work.* She ended up escorting the confused guy back through the front lobby and out the door.

"Mike, you have my explicit permission to leave any meeting which Richard is wasting your or anyone else's time. Even if you're the one presenting, feel free to walk out, I'll cover the rest of it for you. Your time is valuable to Jacqui and me, and we don't want to see it wasted," Kendra said.

"Thanks," Mike said.

Looking down the hall Kendra could see the interviewee waiting for them in the lobby.

"Alright, I need to interview a tech writer, but I'll see you for our one-on-one after lunch," said Kendra.

Truth

Kendra sat behind her desk waiting for Julia. As the CTO of Evolve, Inc., she had the unpleasant duty of letting go employees who weren't working out. Today Julia was one of them.

"Knock, knock. You wanted to see me Kendra?" Julia peeked in the half open door.

"Yes, please come in. Close the door behind you and have a seat," said Kendra.

"What's up?"

"Julia, this concerns your probation period for lying resulting in negative consequences to your work or the company. Another incident has come to my attention. This is now the third time you've lied to another employee with negative consequences to your work or the company."

"What incident?"

"In this last case you were responsible for testing a bug fix implemented by Josh. While you said you did it—I have the chat logs for that conversation— and someone later ran the test cases and found two regressed bugs that would have been found had you run those test cases."

"I swear I ran them."

"We also found no record of the build the fix was in downloaded by you. In fact, there is no record of you downloading any of the recent builds over the last two weeks."

Silence.

Getting to the objective truth had always been important to Kendra. When she was in seventh grade she had Mr. Benson for General Science class. The class introduced students to Biology, Chemistry, and Physics. It was one of the first classes and teachers who truly embraced her penchant for asking questions. Mr. Benson loved her questions. It allowed him to pontificate endlessly on subjects.

"Mr. Benson, when you split a water molecule why are the two parts a gas instead of a liquid?"

"Mr. Benson, why is the sky blue? Why is it any color at all? Why not black like in space?"

"Mr. Benson, why don't antibiotics kill all bacteria?"

Occasionally, Kendra would hit on a question that Mr. Benson didn't know the answer to. He loved those even more.

"That is a wonderful question, Kendra. I have no idea, but you should find out yourself. Keep asking those questions!"

This was a welcome reprieve from one of her elementary school teachers, Mrs. Engels. Mary Engels tired quickly of Kendra's questions and often told her to keep her questions to herself—they were disrupting the class.

"But, I just want to understand why we need to write in cursive instead of print like we practiced the year before", Kendra asked.

"Because you couldn't read the Declaration of Independence without knowing cursive", said Mrs. Engels.

"Why can't we just read the version that is printed in our book?"

"Because I said so, that's why!"

Because I said so, became Kendra's most feared and hated phrase.

Kendra was also bothered when other kids and often adults refused to change their lifestyles when new information was available.

"Nana, you know smoking is bad for you—it's all over the news. Why do you keep smoking?", Kendra once asked her grandma.

"Because I always have, and I don't feel like stopping. Besides, next week they'll tell us smoking is actually safe."

"But, haven't they known for like thirty years that it's bad for you."

"I don't know. Stop asking me so many questions and let me finish this episode of MASH."

As she got older, her questions became more complex and more politically sensitive.

"Grandpa, why don't you and Nana believe in evolution? There's over one hundred years of research supporting it", Kendra asked one Sunday evening during a family dinner. The whole table went silent and her mother's face went completely flush.

"Hahaha! What sort of shit are they teaching you in school these days?", he began.

"Oh, John, watch your language in front of Kendra. She may be naive, but she doesn't need to hear you swear like you were still in the Navy", said Nana.

"For God's sake, Nora, she's seventeen. And if she can ask questions like that, she can hear a 'damn' or 'shit' every once in a while. But, seriously, what happened to sticking with the three R's. Why are these teachers pushing their own liberal agendas? What does a *theory*, mind you, got to do with teaching kids what they need to enter the workforce? Why not just a typing class?"

"Grandpa, although it's *called* the Theory of Evolution, it's been accepted as scientific fact. They teach us it so that we understand the scientific basis for disciplines like Ecology. Ecology is a profession, too, grandpa."

Her curiosity was driven by her passion for truth. She sought truth in everything she pursued. To find out what was *actually* happening, what our world was actually like, and how it actually worked, you had to ask a lot of questions. You had to absorb new information. But, most of all, you could deceive yourself or others. Discovering the truth was no less important in how she ran her business today.

"Julia, one of those regressed bugs was a major security vulnerability. This build was going out to the customer. Fortunately, I have had several of the team members double-checking your work to mitigate risks like this. We caught it this time. But it is clear that we can no longer rely on your word to base team and company decisions. I have to let you go from the company."

Julia let out a sob.

"You do good work most of the time, Julia. However, this is not a good fit for us. I wish you the best in your future pursuits. Jeff from HR is waiting for you in the conference room across the hall. He will explain next steps and escort you out of the office when you're ready."

"Why is this such a big deal to you!"

"Facts and objective reality are the foundation on which rational people make decisions. Without these, our decisions to act, or not, are likely to result in failure.

"If I'm told the plot of land I just purchased is not in a floodplain, I build a house on that land based on that information, and later learn that that information is false, I've put my house and family in danger. I would not otherwise have done that had I been given the facts and truth.

"The same is true for this company. If we make decisions to go into a certain market or release our software, in this case, based on false information, it puts this company in danger.

"This is why we do our research before entering a market, why we run all our test cases before releasing software—to know what we're getting into.

"In the big picture, this is why science in general exists. We must understand our world to make the right decisions. Ignore science, ignore truth, and you might as well be making decisions based on Tarot cards.

"This is why truth is important to me. Without it, we risk losing the things we hold dear."

2

Kendra took the long way home. That was not her original intent.

As she crossed Canyon Boulevard and passed Central Park she had the feeling she was being followed. She stopped and pretended to check her phone, sneaking a peak behind her. The same guy she noticed near the bandshell in the morning and for the past week was walking toward her. This time, however, there was another man with him. Both men appeared to be in their mid-to-late thirties, close cut military-style haircuts, with muscular builds.

Neither of them was looking at her, yet she felt watched somehow. *C'mon, Kendra, why would anyone be following you?* They continued walking past her and stopped at the corner of Arapahoe and Broadway. She decided to cut through the park and test her theory. This was the opposite direction she would go to head home, but if they *were* following her she would be headed in the direction of the university and more people.

As she got to the south side of the park where the path joined Arapahoe Avenue, she looked to the right to see if the two were still there. Only one of the men was there. She decided to play it safe and head east on Arapahoe. After a hundred yards she stopped again and pretended to check her phone again. The two men were gone. *See? No one out to get you.*

She decided to continue east on Arapahoe, opposite the direction of her house and take a longer route home. She thought she could use more exercise anyway. Her obsessive focus on getting Ecolution delivered to her customer and scientists meant she spent a lot more time sitting than she was used to.

Once she hit 17th Street she turned south toward the university. She passed the high school. The boy's high school baseball team was out practicing and, in the field adjacent was the girl's lacrosse team. There was a group of girls huddled together giggling as they watched the boys practice. They burst out laughing as one of the girls impersonated the baseball players. The boys appeared to pay no attention. Kendra knew better. The boys were strutting their stuff knowing full-well they had an audience. Kendra smiled remembering her high school days.

On the far side of the lacrosse field she noticed a man on the path that looked like one of the men she thought was following her earlier. At this distance she couldn't quite tell with any certainty if it was the same man. He was alone. That path would meet up with the sidewalk she was on in about one-hundred yards. If it was the same man, she would soon know.

As the paths drew closer she could no longer see him. A dense swath of forest lay between the sidewalk and the path. Her heart rate increased again as she got closer to the junction. She finally came to the path and looked back over her right shoulder. The man was sitting up against a handrail looking at his phone. It was the Bandshell Man.

She continued down 17th Street at a quickened pace waiting for an opportune time to turn around again. Seventeenth soon merged with University Avenue and she took her chance then. She looked back under the guise of looking at traffic before crossing the busy Avenue. The second man was back. She now knew she wasn't imagining things.

She knew where she was headed now but wanted to make sure she kept in the busiest areas until then. She headed toward the Student Center choosing the busiest paths and streets she could find. She passed Varsity Lake and headed through Norlin Quadrangle where there were plenty of students hanging out on the unbelievably immaculate lawn. Then she headed down the Central Campus Mall to 18th Street and finally cut over toward the Student Center.

Trying to catch her breath, she walked straight over to the student bulletin board. Pretending to read posts, she had a perfect view of the doors she just entered. Her eyes scanned over posts for new roommates, used text books, and even an announcement about a new Denuclearization House opening next year—but her mind registered none of it. She was intently focused on those doors.

After a few minutes she wondered if they had given up. As her hopes were rising, Bandshell Man entered the door. *But, where is the other guy?* She knew the answer.

It had been at least two years since she was last in the Student Center. It was for a recruiting event and she didn't pay much attention to the exits. She assumed the other man was covering another exit. *There's got to be a third exit around here somewhere.*

Kendra turned and headed down the middle of the Center. There were hundreds of students in the main area, so it was slow going at first. As soon as she made it to the first corridor, she bolted down it. She no longer cared to make a scene but knew students probably wouldn't notice anyway. She rounded one corner then another, trying to make her way back to the main hall. She looked back and saw that although he was still behind her, he was far behind. He had obviously chosen not to make a scene himself.

The other exit she knew about was to her left, the one she entered to her right. Without thinking she turned to her left making sure he saw her turn but then dropped down to a crawl beneath the sea of students and turned around back toward her original entrance. She was certain the Other Guy was covering the exit on the left. There were a couple of confused looks from students, but most carried on without paying any attention to her.

As soon as she was far enough around the corner and out of view, she stood up and sprinted toward the doors. She slowed only to exit without a crash. She quickly peeked through the window in the second, external door to make sure she wasn't mistaken about the Other Guy. She didn't see him. Bursting through the door, she took off in a final sprint and headed toward the gap between the Art's Center buildings. She made it to the edge of one of the buildings fifty yards away in only a few seconds and turned the corner.

With her back against the building she tried to catch her breath. Her curiosity got the best of her and she peeked around the corner. As she did, Bandshell Man came out of the doors and looked around. He put his hand up to his ear and appeared to be talking. He paced for another thirty seconds and continued to look around. Then headed back into the Student Center.

She knew she was safe now, but for how much longer. *More importantly*, she wondered, *why were they interested in me?*

Solving Puzzles

The Ecolution team met downstairs from their office just outside the Riddler Rooms. They had finished up the production launch of their product and it was time to celebrate. The whole team and Kendra were there—Mike, Peter, Amanda, Katie, Josh, and Ash.

They were a great team and had all worked together for a few years, apart from Josh. Josh had joined them about a year ago and was just in time. There was a tendency for heroic effort by this team, which is likely what would have happened during the last six months if Kendra didn't know her team well enough. She hired Josh with some lead time to ramp him up before crunch time began. By his six-month mark he was as much a part of the team as if he had always been there.

Apart from Amanda, they were all developers. Amanda was their Product Owner and coordinated and prioritized software requirements for the team.

Unlike most software engineering teams, they did not have any full time Quality Assurance Engineers. Kendra believed that everyone on the team should be interested and responsible for quality. And they all were. They didn't sign off on their own work, but they all wrote automated tests for the features they developed and then passed off the feature to another team member for testing.

They also didn't have a designated technical writer to write their documentation. That was done by the team, as well. It was a lot of work filling multiple roles, but it meant that they were all familiar with a majority of the platform. It also built a lot of trust between each member of the team.

As usual, Peter was providing the entertainment while they were waiting for their time to start.

"No seriously, I turn around and she's just gone. I had turned to grab my drink from the bar, then turned back and there was no one there. So, I looked over the back of the couch and sure enough she's lying on her back on the couch seat cushions, legs sticking straight up—she had totally fallen over the back of the couch. She was still trying to figure out what had happened herself when I looked down at her. We both just burst out laughing!" Peter was talking animatedly.

"Are you all the Evolve team?" a woman's voice said from behind Peter. Peter did a sort of Kramer from Seinfeld surprise move.

"Yep, we're the team," Kendra replied.

"Great. Welcome to the Riddler Room. Follow me and we'll get started."

After listening to the rules of the room, a few jokes from Peter, and handing over their cell phones, which was quite difficult for many of them to relinquish, they all stepped into the escape room. It was a jail cell and they were being locked in. The room was called Chateau d'If. Kendra thought that sounded familiar—*wasn't that the prison in which the Count of Monte Cristo was jailed in the beginning of the book—well, Edmond Dantès before he became the Count,* she thought.

Kendra had been looking forward to this afternoon for a few weeks now. Unfortunately, the events from the previous afternoon still weighed heavily on her mind. After Nikolaj got home, they sat up talking until early into the morning. Neither could think of any reason why someone would be watching her, let alone stalk her through a university campus.

They decided that the best course of action was to report it to the police. She did and got the response she simultaneously expected and dreaded, "thanks mam, we'll keep an eye out for them but if you don't know why they're following you, there's not much we can do about it right now—we're just too busy." Nikolaj didn't allow her to walk to work and she didn't want to. He dropped her off on the mall as he headed into work.

Although the escape room was a treat for her team—a celebration for finishing the first major release of Ecolution—it was also a bit of a treat for her. She enjoyed watching the team work together. It wasn't your typical team with a loud charismatic leader and a bunch of followers. It was a team who took guidance and direction from their implicit leader, Mike, but each had their own strengths which they employed as needed. And none of them took offense or were put off when another of the team shined brighter than they.

Not only a brilliant lead engineer and architect, Mike also had a gift that few other leaders had or used—the gift of listening. Kendra had always been impressed with the way Mike got the team to do the right things at the right times without having to constantly tell them what they should be doing and how. This was exactly what Mike was doing now.

Kendra watched them all as they walked into the room, the door being locked behind them. At first all eyes were looking around surveying the room. One by one they each locked into an object and fanned out. Mike was the last and appeared to be taking inventory of whatever else may give clues that another team member didn't see.

But instead of going to the next available item. Mike walked over to Ash first and started asking a few questions. Although Mike was the one who initiated the talking, Kendra noticed he was soon simply listening. Once he got a good temperature of where Ash was, he went over and sat with Katie and the same sequence of events ensued. He then left Katie and while he went to do the same with Josh, Katie went over and sat with Ash.

Not thirty seconds elapsed before Ash and Katie announced they found something. Ash had been looking through a notebook that had been sitting on top of a small table next to the bed.

"The notebook alludes to something under the bed, but we don't quite know what it's referring to yet," Ash said.

Peter nearly threw himself, comically of course, under the bed, looking for something. There doesn't seem to be anything under here, he yelled.

"Look up," Katie directed.

Peter rolled himself over, so he was now looking up.

"Ah, there's an arrow that points that way," Peter said as he pointed in a direction toward the entrance they came in from which was near the foot of the bed.

"Nothing over there, at least nothing that's obvious," said Amanda.

"This is a little cryptic, but, oh, I think it's French," Katie said. "Anyone know French."

"I studied it a bit in college," Josh said walking over and sitting down next to Katie. "...jambe de lit, uh...," he said thinking. "Lit is bed and jambe is leg, should mean leg of the bed."

"Oh, it's pointing to the leg of the bed," Peter said from beneath the bed.

"Is there anything written on the leg of the bed? Or does it look like it could come off?" Amanda asked.

Peter slid over for a better look but didn't find anything. "No, doesn't look like it."

"Ash, Katie, and Josh, let's get off the bed and see if this leg comes off," Mike said.

They all got off and started lifting the bed. As they did, an old film canister fell out. Peter immediately grabbed it and opened it up.

"A key!" he exclaimed.

They all got excited, but quickly realized they didn't yet know to what.

"Wait," said Ash. "I think I remember something about that in this notebook." She paused looking through the notebook. "Yes, here it is. It didn't make much sense at the time. It reads:

"You can leave at three in the afternoon."

"Uh, it's 3:45 PM now," Amanda said confused.

"There was what looked like part of a sundial on the ledge of that fake window there," Mike said, remembering one of the things that went unnoticed. "Where is that candlestick holder I saw earlier? I wonder if that's all that's missing."

"Here," Peter said, bringing it over.

He put it on the spot Mike was pointing to and with the fake sunlight, the candlestick holder cast a shadow pointing to three.

"Follow this line and see if there's any lock or anything else," Mike said.

They all started looking around along the line from the candlestick holder to the wall. Josh eventually found a brick in the wall directly across from that line that was loose and pulled it out.

"Found something. There's a padlock in here. Who has the key?" Josh said.

"I do," Peter said and made his way to the padlock, inserted the key and turned it. It unlocked, and everyone cheered. "What does this unlock now?"

Josh and Peter began pulling on the few things with a grip and something finally came loose, and part of the brick wall opened like a door.

"Alright, who's first?" Peter exclaimed.

Katie stepped right in but turned right around.

"Bad news guys—it's not the exit, it's another room," Katie said.

"That not so bad, it's only been like twenty minutes," Peter responded, sounding excited for more action.

In the meantime—out of the habit of double-checking the work of another team member—Ash picked up the brick that Josh had pulled out of the wall and was looking over it.

"Looks like this could be relevant, depending on what's in that room," Ash began. "On the backside of this brick is chiseled, 'You must crawl inside the bag to get out of the room'"

"Are you kidding me?" Peter yelled. "There's a body bag in here. Who's going to be the one to climb inside? NOT IT!"

"Oh, jeez, you wuss. I'll do it," Katie said.

"Looks like we need to take a body *out* first," Mike said, as he unraveled the body bag. He began pulling out pieces of a skeleton and handing them to his team around him. Once they got everything out, Katie didn't hesitate and climbed right in.

"That can't be sanitary," Amanda said, almost holding her nose.

"Kinda smells like they wash this. I'm guessing they have to if people actually climb in this thing," Katie said, apparently not at all bothered by the prospect of wrapping around her something that was made to look like it had contained a dead body.

"If there's something in here, I'm going to need a flashlight to see it," Katie said.

"What about the candlestick in the holder? Looked like it might be one of those battery powered ones," Josh trailed off as he ducked back into the previous cell. He came back quickly with the fake candle and had it turned on. "Here it is," he said. One of Katie's hands reached out of the bag for the candle and Josh handed it to her.

"It reads, 'mask the window to reveal the way to your freedom'," Katie said, immediately pulling herself out of the bag. "Yeah, that is a little creepy."

"Mask with what?" Ash asked.

"What about that skull?" Amanda suggested. "That's a type of mask and looks like it would fit well in that window up there."

Peter still had the skull in his hands and walked over to the window, reached up and slid it into the small sill. There was some sort of lens in the skull, because as soon as Peter slid the skull in the window sill, a sharp ray of light shone directly on a picture on the wall above the bed where the body bag lay.

"Weird. I figured it would point to the obvious cell door over there. But I suppose that would be *too* easy," Peter said.

Katie still standing near the bed after emerging from the body bag, leaned over to look at the picture.

"Hmm, nothing obvious *in* the picture," Katie said, as she reached to take the picture off the wall. As soon as she lifted it, they could all see the quarter inch wide and six-inch-long slit in the wall. She peered in and saw something just inside the slit.

"There appears to be some sort of lever in there, but it's too narrow to get a finger in there," Katie said.

"What about this shiv I found on the table over here?" Mike offered, bringing it over. Katie inserted it and flipped the lever up. Everyone except Ash was looking at the wall expecting something to move. Ash, covering other alternatives was looking in other directions from the rest of the team, when she noticed a small drawer open from the small table opposite the wall with the lever. It closed just as she got over to it.

"Do that again, Katie. I think this drawer opened when you moved the lever up," Ash said. Sure enough the drawer opened again, and Ash looked in and found another key.

"I bet this is the final key," she said as she pulled the key out of the drawer. She walked over to the cell door, took a deep breath, inserted it and turned. It unlocked and they all breathed a sigh of relief. She opened the door and the woman who escorted them into the room in the beginning was standing near the entrance. She smiled and congratulated them on a job well done.

"I was ready for more after the first door but have to admit I'm glad we're done this time. Who's up for West Flanders?" Peter exclaimed.

Nods went around. They gathered their phones and other belongings and headed out the door, back onto the Mall, and down the couple of blocks to West Flanders.

2

It was one of their favorite places to hang out after work and their default. They got a table out on the patio and ordered their first round of drinks.

"So, what's next, boss?" asked Ash.

"Well, I know this isn't everyone's favorite job, but we still have a lot of maintenance and support to provide the USGS and USDA as more groups adopt Ecolution. It's not the long-term solution, but something we need to do to ensure its success. Eventually the NITC support staff will ramp up and take over its internal support, long-term," Kendra explained.

"How long is our support contract for?" Ash asked.

"Full-time support will run the year starting in October. We'll still have a low-level of support after that year, but it's only a quarter of someone's time. If we've done a decent job of training the NITC support staff, I hope it will be even less. There's your carrot for training their staff well," Kendra smiled.

Conversations continued between various groups. And Mike and Katie settled into their usual conversation around software engineering and magic. Although they both liked Arthur C. Clarke's third law, "Any sufficiently advanced technology is indistinguishable from magic," they wondered if it didn't also cause some problems in the industry.

"Speaking of the NITC support staff, I was talking with Dave the other day and he kept using the phrases 'beat it into submission' and 'magic happens here'," Katie complained.

"I hear ya. Luckily Dave is not typical of the engineers there," replied Mike.

"Why do people who live in a world where we have all the instructions of an application at our fingertips insist that software does magical things? Jesus, just sit down and read the code—it tells you right there what it does," said Katie.

Kendra had been listening to them and jumped in.

"Nikolaj and I have a very similar conversation about science. We have all this scientific evidence— as you say, Katie, at our fingertips—yet a large part of the population thinks it's either magic or couldn't possibly be true. And I think it all comes down to the junction between complexity and time. As a system becomes more complex, it takes more time to understand it. Depending on your education and background that time will be different. Different people have different tolerances for taking the time to understand a concept.

"Unfortunately, I think it ends up politicizing concepts like global change because it's complex and a large portion of the population doesn't have the time to sit down and understand it. It's easier for them to ignore it and write it off as fiction, since if it was real to them they might need to change the way they live—another time impact. It's much less disruptive to keep business as usual," Kendra said.

"Yeah, I totally see that and how it relates to software. Dave at NITC, who we were just talking about, has about twenty different applications that he and his team support. In the short term, Dave generally has quicker success by randomly poking at something until it works for him. But unfortunately, it means that he doesn't spend the time understanding how that particular feature or software works, so that the next time he comes across it, he's able to fix it right away."

"That's a perfect way of putting it, Katie—it's short term thinking, and in the long-term it's going to bite us in the ass," Kendra concluded.

After the distraction of the escape room and drinks with the team, the events of the afternoon before were long lost to her. Little did she know that on the other side of Pearl Street from West Flanders sat the Bandshell Man.

Ecolution

Around fifty U.S. Geological Survey and U.S. Department of Agriculture employees gathered in the main conference room on the third floor of building six of the Natural Resources Research Center in Fort Collins, Colorado. By Kendra's online conferencing attendee list, it looked like there were another sixty dialed into the conference line. Kendra had worked almost two years for this moment. It was the launch of Evolve's flagship software Ecolution. The software was going to change how scientists collaborated, pooled their data, and analyzed it—it was the next great breakthrough for science and government. It would take climate change research to start with to a whole new level.

Kendra was excited, but also nervous. Dr. Jack Denning, as well as, Dr. Elizabeth Harrison, the Director of the Office of Science Quality and Integrity for the U.S. Geological Survey were both on the line. She had several pleasant conversations with Elizabeth, but Jack was another matter. Kendra could handle tough questions, but Jack's questioning often bordered on the malevolent. She often wondered why Jack continued funding the project that put Ecolution on the map if he despised it so much. There were some personalities she could not quite figure out. Maybe Jack was one of them she never would. He was a highly intelligent person but could be quite the jerk. The contract funds continued to come, so she wrote it off as one of the few things she would never understand.

"Alright, let's get started everyone," Gil broke through the din.

"Kendra is going to take us through the final product demo and introduce next steps for those ready to plug in their data and analysis engines. For those of you who don't know Kendra, she's the CTO for Evolve Incorporated down in Boulder. She's been heavily involved in making sure this product was a success and I'm grateful for her leadership. This was a pipe dream when we first started talking about it almost three years ago. But she and her team have turned it into a reality—a reality that will change the way our teams do science. So, without further ado, Kendra, please take it away."

"Thanks, Gil. The kind words are appreciated, but—not to sound too prosaic—this was a team effort. Not just my team from Evolve, but yours too. As Gil said, we'll take you through the product, diving into details you all will care most about and then we'll dive into how you can integrate the data processing and analysis plugins you've been developing in parallel.

"For those of you who are completely brand new to Ecolution, Ecolution is intended to ease the burden of data validation and storage, and exponentially improve the time it takes to run analyses. By taking advantage of the government cloud infrastructure that you have available to you, your models will run on-demand with much more computer power than you previously had when you were required to purchase your own computer hardware. Early proofs of concept with some of the teams in this room have shown a three-hundred percent improvement in data consistency and quality, and a thousand times improvement in model runtimes."

There was a noticeable amount of excited chatter in the room on this last point. Kendra continued.

"Ecolution is considered a platform for you to add your own data validation algorithms and analysis engines. We'll refer to these as integration points and the code that is written to accomplish this as plugins.

"Now, many of you have heard the team talk about the integration points in mundane detail, but there are still quite a few of you who haven't. For those who've heard this before, please bear with us.

"There are three primary integration points you will be interested in. The first is the data preprocessor plugins. These can be configured to run for particular subsets of data, group of data, or all data. They also run in the context of the data access permissions that each research group sets up for themselves. The preprocessor plugins are intended to be flexible based on specific needs of the research group, office, or department. Some examples include data conversion from Fahrenheit to Celsius or filtering out anomalous values. You can really do anything you need with the data at this point.

"The second integration point allows you to run analysis on the data. These plugins will run in your National Information Technology Center infrastructure, taking advantage of your vast computing resources. For instance, you could run the Northern Region Ecology Lab's EMIT model to calculate greenhouse gas emissions or your own home-grown analysis software.

"The last integration point is for postprocessor plugins. You could do anything from send email notifications to principle investigators when interesting results are found or, again, filter out anomalous results.

"So, let's run through an entire example. Jorge, you run greenhouse gas emission models against data derived from Landsat data, right? And currently you're using a small team of grad students to periodically download the data, scrub it for anomalies, prep it for analysis, run the model on the new data, and check that the results make sense.

"Jorge's team has spent the last few months writing plugins for Ecolution to do all of this for him. They created a simple application that they can run manually or set it to run as a periodic job to check the National Land Cover Database for updated imagery, pull it down if new, and send it to Ecolution. We've been working with their team to create plugins for the integration points we discussed earlier.

"The first plugin filters the data for anomalies, just as the grad students did manually before. At a certain error rate threshold, the plugin will stop processing and send a notification email back to the team detailing the errors found and that the data would not be processed. One of these days we'll get your team on Slack. Otherwise, it will cleanse the data as-needed and send it on to storage and the next step.

"The next step is the analysis plugin. Their plugin will run the greenhouse gas emission model. The final plugin simply sends a summary of the results back to Jorge and his team. From what I have seen of the reports, they also include links back to the detailed results. Jorge, anything you want to add?"

"Absolutely," replied Jorge. "The Evolve team put together a very intuitive and easy to follow interface for these plugins. If anyone needs help getting started, we are happy to answer any questions. Kendra, I know your team is on the hook to provide initial support, but we're excited about this new infrastructure and want to help make it a success."

Richard Knight, the obnoxious know-it-all from the USDA Security team, burst in like a disgruntled version of Kramer just as Jorge finished. Kendra eloquently continued diving into more details of the infrastructure but couldn't help thinking what a jerk Richard was. If she didn't know better, she would think Richard and Jack were in on some dirty little secret together. But Jack would never stoop so low as to mingle with an engineer at Richard's level. Kendra hated having to tell her team to play nice with Richard. "He's a necessary evil," she often told them. Even though Evolve always took the pre-emptive step of hiring a third-party security firm to perform security penetration testing on all their software, their contract stipulated that the USDA also have their own security team assess the software. As Peter from the Evolve development team always said, "whatever, dude" — she knew the software was safe from any major, or minor for that matter, vulnerability.

As Kendra continued, Richard made his way to the opposite side of the room, seemingly making as much noise as possible, then sitting against the wall, computer open typing away as if nothing else was going on in the room.

Peter chuckled quietly behind Mike loud enough to make Mike turn around. "Dude, not during a meeting," Peter laughed.

"Uh, what? Oh, jeez, no. That was he-who-must-not-be-questioned." Mike replied, mildly offended and referring to Richard by their pet name for him. Not that Mike didn't want to pay attention to his boss, but something always seemed to happen when Richard entered the room — and it was usually uncomfortable. Mike once stepped out of a conference room before a meeting started to talk with someone and when he peeked over his shoulder through the small window in the conference room door just in time to catch Richard browsing Mike's notebook. Not that there was anything incriminating in his notebook, *but come on, who does that?* he thought.

"Now my understanding is that Richard has done all the heavy lifting in terms of security for this infrastructure." Jack came through with a comment aimed at diminishing Evolve's role in the project.

Kendra knew she needed to handle this one diplomatically. Though her first thought was to say that Richard was a jackass who spent way too much time working on something that he likely borrowed from an open source security repository. She really did wonder why it took him so long to implement the straight-forward authentication module. She had to give him credit—he was a brilliant engineer and did find a couple of severe security vulnerabilities in Ecolution. Those really should have been caught in code reviews, but she knew they would be caught by the firm doing the penetration testing regardless.

"Thanks for bringing that up, Jack. This is a good time to talk about authenticating against the Data API. For obvious reasons we don't want to open up the Data API to just anyone. We're starting with a simple implementation that will require your in-house applications to authenticate using something called OAuth2 and pass in security tokens with your data requests. Richard, do you want to say a few words about that?"

"Er. Yeah, fine. Each one of your client applications will need to be registered with our authorization server as an application. You will need to supply a few parameters such as a redirect URI. The client id and secret you receive once your app is registered is used to make subsequent requests to retrieve access and refresh tokens…"

Richard continued with excruciating detail for the next few minutes. It almost seemed as if he was talking to himself. He wasn't trying to communicate how to use the authentication mechanism, he was only trying to sound smart. The only people in the room who had any idea what he was talking about were himself, Kendra, and the rest of the Evolve team. Though there were a lot of brains in the room and on the phone, they were all experts in much different fields. Kendra knew this but let him ramble. Let him dig his own grave, she thought. Unfortunately, it would likely come back to her team to help the different teams implement what they needed.

Once Richard finally finished his pontification, Kendra continued. "Thanks, Richard. Because the authentication module was implemented as a global data filter plugin (remember that first integration point we discussed earlier), it will be easier to enhance to broader uses and different authentication mechanisms. For example, if we want to push data directly from measurement probes in the field, we can create an additional authentication mechanism for that."

Kendra was truly proud of Ecolution. They had built an infrastructure that the government could do almost anything with.

"I realize this has been a fairly high-level overview of what Ecolution is and what it does. It's going to be much easier to understand with some hands-on experience. We have all the members of the engineering team with us today—please stand up team. Mike is our lead engineer, along with Peter, Katie, Ashley, Amanda, and Josh. We're going to break out into six separate groups and each one of the team members will lead a mini-workshop on how to integrate with Ecolution. For those on the conference call, I've sent separate meeting invites for each of you to join a different sub-group. They will be going through this on their laptops and sharing their screens, so you can see what they're doing as they go through it. Each one of the sub-groups has a volunteer science team who will present what they do, the data they collect, and the models they run on the data. Then the Evolve team member will step through in a live example, how to write a plugin for validating that data, another for running the model against the data, and another for sending notifications to the team. Any questions?"

After a few questions, everyone went their separate directions to different rooms for the workshops.

2

Mike, Nikolaj, and Nikolaj's team met in one of the smaller conference rooms. The core of Nikolaj's team was made up of Cat and Anir, both had worked for Nikolaj for almost ten years now. There were about a half-dozen other scientists who joined them. Nikolaj was dialing into the conference line.

"Hello, who do we have on the line?" said Nikolaj.

Another half dozen people on the conference line said their names and Mike noticed there were a few more in the online meeting room who chose to stay quiet.

"Great. As Kendra mentioned, I'm going to take the group through a very high-level overview of what data we collect and the model we run against it. Then Mike will take us through some examples of how modules would be written for that data and the models to integrate it all into Ecolution," Nikolaj began.

"For those of you who don't know me, my name is Nikolaj Mikkelsen. I have a joint appointment as a Research Scientist for the USGS and School of Sustainability and Colorado State University. I have two of the core members of my team with me today, Cat Olivier and Anir Bahl.

"Our main area of study is ice shelf stability in Antarctica, specifically on the Filchner-Ronne shelf. We look at ice shelf temperatures at various depths within the shelf and monitor water infiltration and temperatures at those various depths. Probes are placed at these various depths and are connected to a surface level parent probe which also acts as a transmitter to send our data to us daily. The parent probes send the data via a satellite connection to a web service where we can retrieve the data. The probes also store the data locally so in the case of failure, we can later retrieve the data. Obviously, that's not ideal since we can only get down there once a year.

"Part of the brilliance of these probes is that we can configure them remotely. Now that Ecolution is available, we've configured the probes to send the data to the Ecolution web service instead. The data redundancy and backup is much safer than our own labs.

"The temperatures we collect range from just above thirty-two degrees Fahrenheit for water to negative five to negative forty, generally, for ice. We'll see slight variations outside this range but it's rare. We also have a good idea of the different temperature ranges at various depths in and below the shelf, so as we'll see we can add that to the validation module that Mike will show us how to write in a bit.

"Ok, so now the model. We have a home-grown model that we wrote. Cat, what was that written in?"

"Python," Cat replied, looking over at Mike and smiling.

"Right. And it models the changes in ice shelf temperature over time and where water is infiltrating spatially through the shelf. It gives us an overall indication of shelf stability. Questions?" said Nikolaj.

There were a few questions which Nikolaj answered. One of them related to the details of the model, he deferred to Cat and Anir.

"With that, I will turn it over to Mike to discuss Ecolution integration," said Nikolaj.

"As you guys were talking I created this diagram of what data you're collecting, what sort of values you expect, and how it runs through the models. We can refer back to it as I go through writing the modules," said Mike. It was his turn to look over at Cat and give her a smile.

"If I get too technical and start spouting software jargon, please stop me," said Mike.

"Actually, Mike, by the look of the room and who is in the online meeting, I think you're pretty safe. Each one of the teams has at least one person who is familiar with writing code and all the concepts you'll be touching on," said Nikolaj.

"Great. Let's get started with the data validation plugin then. If you take a look at what I have shared on my screen you will see an empty code template. It has everything you need to integrate with Ecolution and tell the software that this is a data validation module. Whatever code you need for your data validation can go here, inside this method. If you have a bunch of supporting code or just want to keep this simple, you can either reference that other module that your code is in or place it in the same module—whichever you prefer.

"For Nikolaj and his team's purpose, we'll write a small function to throw a data validation exception if, as Nikolaj mentioned earlier, the temperature data comes back lower than negative forty degrees Fahrenheit or above thirty-five. Good enough for demonstration purposes anyway," said Mike as he finished typing the function.

"Of course, your actual code will be much more complicated than this, but hopefully this gives you the idea. To show you how it works, I'll compile the code and copy the resulting module into the Ecolution plugins directory. The Ecolution software will recognize there is a new module in the directory and try to load it and see if it recognizes any integration points. Once it loads we can then send in data to see how it responds.

"Cat sent me some sample data yesterday, so I have it here. We'll take a part of this data file and send a request to Ecolution to process it. Some of these data points we know fall outside that data validation range we just defined, so we expect at least some of the data to fail validation," said Mike typing as he was talking. He ended by hitting the enter key.

"Ok, we sent the data and will give it a second or two to run. Alright, so now it ran, and you can see in the response that we have a few exceptions. Most of the data was successfully added to the system, but a few data points failed. For your own systems, you could fairly easily write some code to notify you if some data failed to import or do some other post-processing to correct the anomalies and resubmit, depending on what you needed to do.

"So, that's data validation. The other two integration points follow the same pattern with slightly different code templates which tell Ecolution those plugins are for different integration points. The more complicated part of the next integration, which runs your model, is that your model must be installed on a USDA virtual machine so that Ecolution can run it and spin up more instances as it needs. We'll cover that later though. For now, you just need to know to start with this code template and change the configuration here to point to your model tell Ecolution what else it needs to know to run the model.

"Nikolaj installed the model on my laptop the other day, so I'll just write these few lines here to configure the necessary parameters. Before we run this part, let's finish the final plugin as well. You could do almost anything you wanted with the final plugin—send an email with the results to your boss, run a different model that requires output from the first, whatever you needed. For now, we'll send a text to Nikolaj when the model finishes with a simple message that tells him whether or not the results were expected or outside the normal range," said Mike again as he was typing all that out.

"Alright. So, now we have all three modules written. I have them compiled now and copied over to the plugins directory. We'll give Ecolution the chance to recognize those. And now that it has, we'll send a request to run the data we previously imported through the model and post-processing step.

"That will take a minute or two to complete, but once it's finished we should hear a..." Mike was interrupted by a ding on Nikolaj's phone.

"Apparently, it's complete," Nikolaj said holding up his phone to show the rest of the people in the room the message he received from Ecolution.

A message from Ecolution: your model run is complete and shows results consistent with an unstable ice sheet.

Debate

Dr. Jeff Anderton was one of Nikolaj's best friends and colleagues in the department. He poked his head into Nikolaj's office overlooking the University's greenhouses, interrupting him with a cheery, "yo, want to grab a coffee?"

"Of course. Sweet Temptations?"

"I think they're closed now that the semester is over. How about Lory?"

"Yeah, that's fine."

Neither really cared where they ended up. They enjoyed the break from their current activities of peer reviewing paper submissions and instead debating some topic. As they made their way through Monfort Quadrangle between the Plant and Animal Sciences buildings, their conversation turned to their favorite topic—the politics of science.

"Jeff, you know my view on this, when the process of science becomes political, it's no longer science. If you want to ignore the results of science to create ignorant policies, well that's your decision to put people in peril. But leave the process of science alone. We, or at least *I*, separate ourselves from policy decisions so we remain emotionally unattached to our findings. Otherwise we risk tainting our interpretation of the data," said Nikolaj.

"Sure, but we have all this knowledge and experience accumulated over the years that unless we promote it, it provides no impact. It's like creating this awesome new product and letting the potential market decide for themselves whether to buy it—that just doesn't happen," said Jeff.

"Simple solution, hire a marketing department then. But leave me out of it. Listen, Kendra complains about this all the time. When she played a herp in her previous life in Glacier National Park, she worked with a guy who almost outright said that he collected data to keep the grizzly on the Endangered Species List. That's just plain wrong. I know that's an extreme example and not necessarily what you're promoting, but that bridge starts to form when we try to serve both masters. We separate the process of science from that of making policy, so we don't end up like the idiot Kendra worked with. That's just bad science. In fact, it's not science at all. We're not scientists to save anything, we're scientists to find the truth. And if that truth is that a species or ecosystem is fine, then we need to live with that. If it's not doing well, that's ok too. We report our findings and those who make policies can make informed decisions about those policies," said Nikolaj.

"Sure, I get that. But, Niki, you and I both know that many of those policy makers often don't make those *informed* decisions. They ignore our data and results and make whatever dumbass decision they need to make immediate political wins. Doesn't matter if it's going to ruin long term impacts to an ecosystem or even our own long-term sustainability on this planet.

"People do this every day. A lot of times they don't know they do, but they do. They have the facts in front of them and they can either choose to use those facts to make a decision or ignore them and live with the consequences. The real problems arise when you're making decisions for a large group of people based on your beliefs instead of factual data.

"Gore hit it spot on—it's an assault on reason. It's an attack on everything that's good in the world. Gore put it this way, 'Simplicity is always more appealing than complexity, and faith is always more comforting than doubt. Both religious faith and uncomplicated explanations of the world are even more highly valued'. Kahneman said something similar when he discussed attribute substitution. Essentially, if people feel a question is too difficult, they will often substitute an easier question that they *can* answer, even if it doesn't relate to the original question. I'm paraphrasing, but you get the gist.

"Human nature or not, I can't just sit back and watch this train wreck with the knowledge that some bus load of innocent people sits on the tracks ahead. I'm going to let that conductor know what's ahead," said Jeff.

Nikolaj couldn't help but think that many of the students around them assaulted reason nightly—and daily. Bringing himself back.

"Jeff, many of our current 'train conductors' don't give a rat's ass that there is a bus load of innocent people they're going to destroy. As long as their train keeps going, they really just don't care...at least as long as they're on that train. For some of them, it isn't long.

"The fact is everyone has their own reality, it's unavoidable and, to some extent, makes life interesting. You and I, when we're met with new facts we adjust our reality, right? Others either filter out facts that don't meet their reality or bend them, so they do. Even you and I do that at times. We have cognitive bias to thank for that. We just have to be careful and follow sound scientific process, so it doesn't leak into our work—which is also why we have peer reviews. Science isn't about proving a point, it's about finding the truth...whatever it may be," said Nikolaj.

"Yeah, I get ya. I just don't trust what's in between our science and their policy. Did you see the debacle at the International Agency for Research on Cancer and what they did with their report on glyphosate?" said Jeff.

"No, what happened?" asked Nikolaj.

"Apparently an early draft leaked out and when someone compared it with the final draft they found that studies that found glyphosate was not carcinogenic were pulled out of the final report—in several places. And the IARC claims that their deliberations shouldn't be transparent to the public. That's like writing a scientific paper without including your methods—how can someone determine its validity if they don't know how or where the data and conclusions came from?" said Jeff.

"Are you kidding me? Yeah, that's ridiculous. It's also one of the reasons policy makers don't often trust us—because of people like that in the IARC, policy makers think we're a bunch of slimeballs. This is another reason we shouldn't be advising on policy," said Nikolaj.

"Unfortunately, the European Union is set to make a policy decision based on that report that could very negatively affect farmers across Europe. But, how else would government entities make these decisions. It's not like a senator or some world leader is going to sit down and sift through a hundred studies on glyphosate to make an informed decision. They need a scientist or group of scientists to sift through those studies for them and give them a summary of all of them," said Jeff.

"Absolutely. And I think—for the most part, with this possible exception—that works. At least in that case you have a *different* set of scientists who are trained in the scientific method making objective decisions to summarize the data—basically a meta-analysis along the same lines as our own base research. The *difference* is that the methods of their meta-analysis are not open for review, as the methods of our analysis have to be in order to publish our results. I think that's the key and maybe a rule that should be followed—policy makers can't accept scientific input unless the methods of its analysis are completely transparent," said Nikolaj.

"Are we coming to an agreement on something?" said Jeff.

"You and I actually agree on most things. We just tend to talk about the things we don't agree on. I just assumed we were keeping ourselves in check," said Nikolaj.

"Yeah, I'm on board. Speaking of keeping each other in check—I have a class to teach and you need to get back to work. Just because you're a Doctor of Philosophy doesn't mean you are paid for philosophizing," said Jeff.

"Not true. What are you about to go do in your Foundations of Ecology class?" said Nikolaj.

"Well played," said Jeff.

Discovery

Kendra sat on her couch listening to Dobrinka Tabakova's Concerto for Violoncello and Strings. She loved its geometric sounds and felt it helped her mathematical mind think. She couldn't understand why the symphonies in the area never played it. If they had a hope of bringing in young people to their concert hall, Tabakova's Concertos could do it.

Coda was laying by her side in one of his rare moments of quiet. Although eleven years old her black lab was otherwise always ready for action. She got him at the Humane Society of Western Montana in Missoula when she was a grad student at U of M more than ten years ago. They thought he was likely mixed with something else but didn't know. She surmised hound of some sort with those big floppy ears and deep howl you could hear from miles around. Kendra also figured he was of the American Black Lab variety with those long legs and a spirit that seemed to have no end. English Black Labs were damn cute too but ran out of steam years earlier than their American counterparts.

She was seething over the recent Bitserv memo. What kind of idiot would write such a thing. It sounded like the drivel the Nazis used to justify genocide. Her theory was that it was written by some male engineer who hasn't left the Bitserv campus since he graduated college three years ago and his girlfriend recently broke up with him. This was his revenge—or so he thought before the dumbass was fired. Now he was off campus.

Her thoughts were interrupted as Nikolaj opened the door.

"Hey, hon," she said automatically.

"God, I hate that drive," he replied. They both loved Boulder and when Kendra and Jacqui decided to start Evolve together they settled in Boulder. With Nikolaj working in Fort Collins, it meant he had to commute the 55 miles to and from the CSU campus most days.

"You look as if something more is bothering you than the drive," Kendra commented.

"Yeah, there is. Something I can't quite wrap my head around. But let's go grab some dinner. We can talk along the way."

Kendra knew what this called for, "Pasta Jay's?"

"Amen," Nikolaj answered.

As they walked toward Pearl Street, Nikolaj described what he'd been seeing, or not seeing as the case happened to be.

"Ever since we started pushing our data and analysis through Ecolution we're no longer setting results consistent with climate change. Maybe things are course correcting? But that doesn't seem likely based on what field crews are reporting," Nikolaj started.

"Well I guess that's why you collect quantitative data and follow a strict data collection protocol, right? To ensure you eliminate or at least minimize human biases."

"Yeah, exactly. But why would it change all of a sudden? Anything Ecolution might be doing to our data?"

"If I recall correctly, you guys didn't implement a data filter that would be changing data values, right? Otherwise, the Ecolution infrastructure itself doesn't modify the data in any way. It stores and retrieves it as is."

"Yeah, mostly right. We did implement a data filter, but it's super rudimentary. It only throws out anomalous values beyond a fairly large range."

"Have you retested to make sure it works as expected."

"Yeah, we took your advice and worked with Mike to write some unit tests that run every time we push code to our GitHub repository."

"Well, listen to you. You sound more like a software engineer every day. I'm proud," Kendra beamed.

"Ha, I bet you are. But don't forget your own roots."

"Once a herp, always a herp! Anyway, hmm. That does sound strange."

"I know Evolve isn't responsible for making our stuff work. Just wondering if you had any ideas."

"No, absolutely. I do want to make sure you guys are successful though. If you are, we are. Have you run old data you know showed the results you'd expect through the same model running in Ecolution?"

"No, not yet. The migration team hasn't gotten to our data yet. "

"How about pulling the data from Ecolution and running the analysis locally."

"Ah, that we haven't tried. We'll give that a try tomorrow. Thanks, hon. I can always count on you to help me figure this stuff out."

"Give Mike a call in the morning and he can help you with the API requests needed to pull down the data, and how to transform it to the format you need."

After reaching the restaurant and ordering their favorite bottle of Cabernet Sauvignon the conversation veered into less serious territory. Once Nikolaj had his favorite dish sitting in front of him, Rigatoni Al, along with two glasses of wine down the gullet, he couldn't care less about his long commute.

Censorship

Dr. Tom Lloyd, a USGS researcher at the Northwest Climate Science Center, sat across from his boss Bob Reynolds. Both were visibly frustrated. Tom held in his hand a memo from the Deputy Director outlining the new publication guidelines which dictated that the term 'climate change' was no longer to be used in any USGS publications.

"Tom, all they want is to tailor government documents to follow their message," Bob pleaded.

Tom was in no mood to be convinced of anything. At the age of fifty-two, he had strong beliefs of right and wrong. And this was without a doubt, wrong.

"Bob, I love working for you, please believe that. But you can be so naive sometimes. You're not getting this. They are censoring our work. They are telling us to modify our results based on *their own beliefs*, not facts, beliefs. They are destroying the scientific process to accomplish their agenda. We're no longer doing science, we're writing propaganda for them. I've turned into their marketing copy editor."

Bob appreciated the work Tom produced and was frankly amazed with his brilliance. But, he knew Tom could be hard-headed.

"And once again you're taking things to extremes. All the past administrations have done this. This is business as usual. You need to remember who you work for," Bob retorted

"Irrelevant bullshit. As soon as you enforce this you can change our tagline to, Propaganda for a Changing World. This Center can be renamed to the Northwest POTUS Marketing Center instead of the USGS Northwest Climate Science Center. There will be no science being done here.

"I'm sure people wonder why the government is in the business of doing science in the first place. Just as we have three branches of government to check each other, we also have scientific branches to keep check on the truth. As soon as the executive branch dictates how we do our work, the check on truth is lost and we're another step closer to a failing democracy.

"I may get a paycheck from the government, but I am tasked to perform science. You are telling me the two are currently incompatible. If you edit out so much as one 'climate change' reference from my paper, I'm out."

The following week, neither Bob nor Tom came to work at the Northwest Climate Science Center. And neither ever returned.

2

Mark Sanderson, an MS candidate from Oregon State University, spent his summer on the Central Oregon coast in the Bayview Oxbow and Starr Creek Preserves under the supervision of Dr. Alice Hooper. He was finishing up his field work, collecting data on coastal marshes for his thesis. Dr. Hooper was a leading expert in the field and a clear authoritative source.

Alexander Morrison, a tech billionaire who now funded climate change research, scheduled a visit to the Preserves to meet with Alice and her team to better understand changes in coastlines and how it relates to climate change, and see if the Morrison Foundation could be of any help. However, Alice was informed that as an Environmental Protection Agency employee, she was not to meet with Morrison.

Mark was to meet with Morrison in her place and was given a list of talking points he could discuss, along with a list of things he was forbidden to discuss. The former list included the biological history of the area. The latter list included climate change and coastline degradation. He would be accompanied by someone from the DC office of whom neither he nor Alice had ever heard. For fear of ruining his career path, he stuck closely to the script.

3

Dr. Janet Turnball, University Director of the Northeast Climate Science Center at the University of Massachusetts, was on her way to the airport for a flight to Spain for the annual United Nations Climate Change Conference. She was excited to see some of her friends and colleagues, but also a little nervous knowing there were so many heads of state there, as well.

As she pulled into the airport parking area her phone rang. It was the department secretary.

"Hi Terry," she said, answering the phone.

"Hi Janet. Uh, I know this is weird, but I just got a call from someone from the USGS. They told me your request to go to COP was denied."

"Oh, Jesus. It's a little late now. I'm at the airport, have my ticket and reservations in Barcelona. I'm not backing out now."

"That what I told the guy, but he said that you wouldn't be able to board the plane—that your ticket was cancelled along with the rest of your reservations."

"Well, whatever. They probably got something mixed up. Sorry you had to deal with him, Terry. Anyway, I'm on my way to COP regardless. You have a good week and I'll see you next."

"You too, Janet."

Janet hung up the phone and parked. Then she grabbed her suitcase and headed to the terminal. After standing in the security line for a half hour, she approached the TSA guard and handed him her passport and scanned her boarding pass on her phone. It made a jarring beep and the guard looked a little surprised. He was reading something on a console and then paused.

"Ma'am, I'm sorry, but it appears your boarding pass is not valid."

Root Cause Analysis

When Nikolaj got in the next morning, he immediately sat down with Cat and Anir and updated them on his conversation with Kendra.

"Kendra recommended we pull the most recent data out of Ecolution and run it through our model on a local machine. It may give us the same results, but at least we'll know whether or not there is something with running the model in the Ecolution infrastructure.

"Cat, please give Mike from Evolve a call and figure out how to pull the data from the API."

"Sure," Cat replied.

"In the meantime, Anir, please set up one of our servers here to run the analysis once the data is ready," Nikolaj continued.

"Will do," replied Anir. "I should have that set up by the end of the day."

"And I'll see how involved the data pull and conversion is and let you know when that piece will be ready. I should know soon after talking with Mike, maybe later this morning," Cat included.

After looking through the API documentation, Cat gave Mike a call.

"Hey Mike, it's Cat over at SoS," Cat said.

"Oh, hey, Cat. What's up?" Mike was pleased to hear from her. Any chance he could get to chat with Cat was a good day.

"Kendra may have already told you this, but we're trying to figure out if our models running in Ecolution are giving us accurate results. Nikolaj doesn't seem to think so and I think he's right," Cat started.

"Yeah, Kendra did give me a heads-up about that," replied Mike.

"So, we'd like to pull our data out of Ecolution using the API so we can run the model locally to see if we get the same results. I've started reading the docs and setting up a client to make the requests, but I have a few questions," Cat continued.

"Absolutely. Why don't we jump in my GoToMeeting and you can share your screen. I'll take you through it". Mike was more than happy to help.

They spent a few minutes going through the steps involved and what parameters the requests needed to get the data Cat was looking for. After that Mike tried helplessly to wrangle Cat into a conversation about her weekend and what she was up to, but Cat was too focused on the task at hand.

"Listen, I should get these data downloads started so that Anir can start with the analysis this afternoon. But I really appreciate your help. Mind if I give you a call later if I run into a snag?"

"Not at all. Please do. And if it makes it any easier, I'm happy to come up tomorrow to help," Mike said hopefully.

"Thanks, I may take you up on that."

They hung up and Cat immediately got to work generating the requests she needed and kicking them off. By the time she returned from lunch she had all the data they needed, and she began the conversion process from the data format the API returned and the convoluted, old-school flat file format the model needed. Scripting data conversion routines was something Cat was well-versed in and had something going in a half hour. It would just take much of the rest of the day to process.

By four that afternoon Cat and Anir's work had finally converged and they were ready to kick off the model runs.

2

Nikolaj, Cat, and Anir came in a little earlier the next morning, eager to see the results. They poured through the results, comparing them to the results from Ecolution. They all matched—every output variable was exactly the same.

"Huh, well, looks like the model running in Ecolution is consistent with what we'd expect," said Anir.

"Yeah," replied Cat and Nikolaj in unison.

"But you don't sound convinced, Nikolaj," Anir replied slowly.

"I can't say that I am. The results all look right. They match what I would expect from the input. But

I don't understand why results would suddenly start changing." Nikolaj was clearly puzzled.

A puzzled Nikolaj was often not pleasant. He'd forget to eat, would sit at his desk too long, and not get up and move around. That would affect his mood. And although he knew all of this would happen, he still wouldn't stop the inevitable. The inevitable also involved him figuring it out, no matter how tough a problem. It just frustrated him that it took him so long to solve it. That had the somewhat dysfunctional effect of encouraging Anir and Cat to either avoid him or dive in and help at heroic levels. Cat and Anir gave each other a knowing look.

3

"Hi Mike, got a sec?" asked Cat, sounding frustrated. She and Anir talked through what might be happening after Nikolaj wandered off to his desk to submerge himself in the problem.

"Of course," replied Mike with piqued excitement.

"We ran the model with the data we pulled from Ecolution, but still got the same results…," she started.

"But Nikolaj isn't convinced there's still not a problem," Mike interrupted.

"Exactly," Cat answered.

"Why don't we screen share and I can show you the flow of data through the system. I know you know all this already, but maybe stepping through it again will generate some ideas," said Mike.

"Sure, worth a try," Cat answered.

"Alright, let me know when you see my screen."

"Yep, we're good"

"OK, the data from your remote probes come in here via this web service. The web service has an intercepting filter that ensures the request includes a valid access token. Now your data is configured to go through this data filter that you and Anir wrote. It essentially throws out anomalous values that aren't really possible, like a stream temperature reading of 415 degrees—not possible. I believe we worked together to write unit tests for that filter. Unless you've rewritten any code since then, it's safe to say that filter is working as intended. We can rule out a problem there.

"There are no other data filters at this stage, so your data is saved to the database and a job is created to run your model. The model runs, producing results that are passed to the email notification plugin, which forwards a formatted report of the results to you, Nikolaj, and Anir. The email plugin doesn't change the data in anyway," Mike paused.

"And that makes sense because the results we receive from the Ecolution emails match the results we saw this morning," Cat said.

"I have to be honest, I just can't see what might be going wrong. Are you sure there really is something wrong?" Mike asked.

"To be honest, I'm not one hundred percent sure myself. But I'm with Nikolaj, something isn't adding up. It just doesn't make sense that pre-Ecolution our probes were sending us data that indicated conditions consistent with climate change. And, now our models are telling us the opposite.

"Well, I appreciate you walking me through this. It's getting late though, and I need to go grab something to eat" Cat went on.

"Yeah, no problem," replied Mike.

"Actually, want to grab a bite somewhere and talk through it some more? Good food always helps me think," Cat asked.

Mike couldn't believe his luck. He wanted to jump out of his seat and do a little dance. Being in the office, he settled for, "ah, yeah, I'd love that...I mean, yeah, definitely up for that."

The stuttering didn't get past Cat and she suddenly got a little flustered too, "ok, I'll see you there then. Bye."

"Wait," Mike said, "where did you want to meet?"

"Oh, sorry, I'm apparently too hungry to think. Since you're down in Boulder and I'm up here in Fort Collins, something in the middle. I know Loveland is a longer drive for you, but there's a great restaurant in downtown that I love called Casandra's. You mind driving a little further and meet there?" Cat said.

"Not at all. See you there in about forty-five minutes."

Mike just about launched out of his chair toward the door. Kendra was just in time to catch him.

"Where are you going in such a hurry? I didn't realize this place was so hard to work for that you couldn't wait to leave every day," Kendra snarked.

"Oh, ah, yeah. Just got off the phone with Cat. We're meeting in Loveland to see if we can't tease out the problem they're having with the results coming out of Ecolution," Mike replied, somewhat embarrassed. He knew Kendra could see right through him.

"I see. Well, enjoy your date...I mean meeting" said Kendra, continuing with the snark.

At this point Mike was as red as a beet and so flustered he didn't bother trying to retain any self-respect he had. As Mike slunk out the door, Kendra turned back to her office to grab her things and head home. If Nikolaj's team was struggling with a problem, she knew it was going to be a long night.

4

Kendra waited for Nikolaj to get home. She had prepared his favorite meal of Røget laks—cold smoked salmon on bread, with shrimp, topped with lemon and dill. She thought it quite disgusting and made herself a grilled cheese with guacamole and jalapenos. Cold smoked salmon on bread with shrimp—sounded like a bachelor came home one day after a long day of work and that was all he had left in the refrigerator, so he threw it together and ate it without bothering to heat it up.

Didn't the Canadians have something like that, too, she thought. Right, poutine—mixture of cheese curds, French fries, gravy, and fatback. Or was that last ingredient an American addition? She had been told that the Americans butchered it by creating variations of it. And apparently the cheese curds are *squeaky* cheese curds according to the Canadians.

Nikolaj never takes care of himself when he's tackling a tough problem, she thought. She wanted to make sure he kept healthy enough to think straight, but there was also a bit of self-preservation in the preemptive meal. Not that Nikolaj was mean or abusive—just a bit hard to be around. She knew that Cat's dinner with Mike would be a nice reprieve from a day with Nikolaj struggling with a problem.

5

Mike knew Friday traffic up the Diagonal between Boulder and Longmont would be a mess, so he took the backroads up to Loveland instead. It was much more peaceful anyway. There was some construction on 83rd—probably replacing the culvert under the road again for the fifth time, he thought— so he cut over to 95th via the dirt road Yellowstone. It was a little longer, but he would get to drive by that odd-looking cottonwood along the road that had been sheared off ten feet from its base from a tornado. Took a double-take the first time he saw that, and it still made him wonder just how powerful a force that tornado was that took the top off a tree that was well over two feet wide.

By the time he made it to Casandra's, he was a few minutes late. Cat had figured that might happen and wasn't upset about it. Although it didn't hurt that she had a mostly empty martini sitting in front of her. Mike felt an awkward moment as he walked up—*do I hug her as if I'm on a date or shake hands as if we're in the office? Jeez, dude, get it together—she asked you here to talk about work,* he thought. Just as he got to the table, she stood, leaned over and gave him a gentle, we're-more-than-just-business-acquaintants hug. Mike, always the over-thinker couldn't help himself though—*was it a more-than-just-friends-too hug? Again, dude, get yourself together,* he thought.

"Have you ever been here?" Cat asked.

"No, this is a pretty cool place. Didn't expect this in downtown Loveland," Mike responded.

"Well, you're in for a treat. They have great tapas, entrees, drinks, *and* art and architecture. A guy by the name of Andy Martin has done most of it. And the photos were taken by a Sarah Davis. Some of the materials they used came from a place called John Harper's Hardware and Recycling south of town. It's this super-cool recycled materials hardware store. They have just about any building material you could find at a big-name hardware store, but it's all reclaimed—old doors, windows, light fixtures. If I ever build my own house or a cabin, I have a feeling I'll spend a lot of time in that place.

"Anyway, this table was made from re-using materials from a local utility company. That platform over to your right where those other tables are, is made from a 1950's train boxcar."

All of Mike's anxiety melted away as Cat was talking. He didn't even notice.

"Huh, that's cool. These beams are beautiful. I could imagine those fitting in well in a modern cabin. There's a cabin plan I've been eying by an Alex Thompson out of California, who built a small-ish cabin for a couple in the Sierra-Nevada range who needed something that could be protected by the harsh winters and potential fires up there. It has a metal roof and exterior, with these sliding doors that cover the windows and doors when they're away. The metal makes for a bit of a modern look, but these worn beams would look great on the inside.

"Take a look at this," Mike clearly had spent a lot of time thinking about this cabin and had pictures of it on the ready in his PinIt account. Cat thought, *huh, a man with taste, intelligent, and not bad to look at*. Wait, this last thought took her by surprise.

"Anyway, sorry. You asked to meet to talk about the potential issue with Ecolution," Mike changed direction, remembering why they were there.

"Oh, right. We're really stumped and could use your guys' expertise. Consider this a support request," Cat said.

"Let me just try to talk this out again to make sure I have everything correct. Since moving to

Ecolution, your model runs are no longer producing the same type of results that pre-Ecolution runs did."

"Correct."

"But pulling your data out of Ecolution and running the model on your own computers give the same results as the results coming out of Ecolution."

"Right."

"And the only data filter module you implemented has been tested and you believe that would have no adverse effects on the data."

"Right. You helped us create some tests—I think you called them automated unit tests—to make sure it was operating correctly. And we have run a representative sample of our past data through it to make sure it filters the data as we would expect. We re-ran those tests again today, just to make sure."

"Ok, good. Good, but weird. At this point with so few teams starting to use it, there shouldn't be anything else that is interfering with your data. But that's got to be it since you essentially proved that the model is running as expected within Ecolution. There has got to be something that is modifying your data. Do you know what the original data was that was sent to Ecolution?"

"No, the probes that send the data, also store it locally. But we can't get to it until someone physically goes out to the probes for maintenance."

"And when does that happen next?"

"Not until Nikolaj goes down there in January for his annual trip. You know they are in Antarctica, right?"

"Wow, you guys do some crazy shit! Yeah, I guess I knew that in the back of my mind from hearing Kendra talk about what Nikolaj and your team does. I apparently never *really* thought about it much. There's no way to get that data, then, anytime soon."

"Probably not, but it depends on who is down there right now. Could be someone Nikolaj knows could pull the data storage devices on one, but we don't have any replacements down there—we'd end up losing data until it was replaced. Nikolaj won't want to do that."

"Do you have any old data sets that you know produced the results you were seeing before?"

"Yeah."

"Ok, we can do something with that, I think. Tomorrow, find that data. What we'll try to do is send it to Ecolution using the same web service endpoint that the probes are sending to. Then we'll try to pull that data back out and see if it was changed at all," Mike said.

"Makes sense. But, if it is changed, what would that mean. I thought the only thing that would change our data is our data filter module plugin, and we've ruled that out."

"Agreed, it's probably not your plugin. But we've safely ruled out everything else. We need to rule out any other factors, as well. At least we'll have more data points to work with."

"It does make me feel better knowing there's at least one more thing to try. And now I can truly enjoy my chocolate cake!" Cat said, licking her lips.

"This food is good and thanks, I really enjoyed hanging out—even if we did end up talking about work."

"Me too," said Cat as she looked up and smiled at Mike. It was a content smile.

6

Mike's heels were just about clicking in the air as he arrived back at his apartment near Flatiron Crossing in Broomfield, southeast of Boulder. He couldn't afford the housing in Boulder like the house Kendra and Nikolaj had. It was nice out where he was anyway. He had great views of the Flatirons hovering above Boulder and a lot of open space to use on his usual afternoon runs after work. He didn't mind missing his run tonight—he thoroughly enjoyed his dinner with Cat. Now he needed to figure out how to arrange for another one. The smile she gave him at the end of dinner suggested it might not be as difficult as he first imagined.

In fact, maybe even tomorrow night. As they had left the restaurant he suggested that he come up to her office tomorrow and they work directly on the problem together. She readily accepted, and they arranged to meet at the office at nine.

7

Nikolaj strolled into the office around a quarter past nine and saw Mike in Cat's office—them both working away at a problem. The same problem he presumed as the one he had been working on with Cat and Anir. The same problem Kendra suggested they allow Cat and Mike to work out themselves. As difficult as it was going to be for Nikolaj to let go, he knew Kendra was right to allow them to take the lead. First, neither of them needed to be micromanaged. And, second, if they solved it together, it might help evolve a growing relationship.

Nikolaj continued walking into his own office.

"We have your old data. Now let's reformat it so we can send it to the web service," Mike began. He opened a text editor, one she had started using she noticed him using it while screen sharing one day. With a few shortcut keystrokes it suddenly turned into a format Mike referred to as JSON.

"Ok, now we can use the web service client you were using to post the data to Ecolution." A few more shortcut keystrokes and he had the web service client program running and a couple of requests templated out.

"Do you have the client ID and secret values available that you use to authenticate against Ecolution," Mike asked.

"Yeah, they're in the first tab of the text editor you were using," Cat answered.

Cat noticed that Mike hadn't touched the mouse at all. Everything he did was on the keyboard without his hands leaving the same position.

"Just curious, but why don't you use the mouse?" Cat asked.

"This is going to sound extremely nerdy, but it's to save time. Changing back and forth between the keyboard and a mouse is inefficient both in time and can even sometimes cause a cognitive context change. Every time you make that shift you can lose a little bit of focus and time. Over a whole day it actually adds up to a lot of time—upwards of fifteen minutes a day or eight days a year."

"Yes, that does sound extremely nerdy," Cat smiled. "I thought I was the scientist."

"You are, but the application of science isn't limited to nerds like you," Mike snarked back.

"Fair"

"Now that we have the client ID and secret, we can use those to get an access token for subsequent requests that need authentication." Mike makes a few more keystrokes.

"And now we can copy this token over to the data post request and copy the formatted data into the body of the request. Submitting. And this will take a bit of processing time." Mike waited about twenty seconds, then opened another request tab.

"Given the identifier returned from the previous request, this next request will check the status of the data processing so we'll know when it's ready to be retrieved," Mike hit the submit button.

"And it looks like it's ready, so we'll use this same ID to request the filtered data," Mike again opened a new request tab, copied in the identifier, and hit submit.

"OK, here's the data returned from the request. This data is what was validated and filtered from your original data that we made the original request with. It's also what will go into the model run that should be setting up and running soon. I'll copy this over to your text editor and split the windows, so you can compare your original data with the filtered." Mike made a few more keystrokes and the data was sitting side by side with Cat's original data.

They both stared for several minutes looking through the data. Cat scrolled the editor windows up and down. She was in disbelief.

"Why are these values changed? It doesn't make sense. All the original values were valid and should have remained the same. Are you sure this is the same dataset?" Cat asked.

Mike flipped back to the web service client and flipped through the tabs, double checking his requests.

"Yep, that's the filtered data from the original data set we sent in," he replied.

"Look at the temperature data for instance. They're all off by just a couple of degrees—all the filtered values are consistently lower than the original. But, why?"

"No idea. Have you run these exact values through the automated tests that check your filter?"

"No," she replied.

"Let's do that really quick. Where do you keep those tests?"

Cat pointed to the directory in file explorer window that held the tests. Mike's magic hands opened the folder, then one of the files in a text editor, copied the data over, then opened a command line window and typed in the command to run the tests. A bunch of text flew up and scrolled through the window within the short span of two seconds. At the end of the text read:

```
=== TEST EXECUTION SUMMARY ===
Total: 4
Errors: 0
Failed: 0
Skipped 0
Time: 0.145s
```

"Given what you said earlier, I set the expected filtered values to be the same as the original values— meaning that the test expected the filtered data to be exactly the same as the original data."

"That proves it's not our filter conclusively then."

"Correct."

"That rules out virtually everything then. What are we missing?" Cat asked, visibly frustrated.

"The security module. It's the only other module that has access to the data. It's not supposed to do anything with the data, but it's the only possible explanation."

"Why would the security team want to modify the data? Isn't that module only intended to authenticate and authorize requests?"

"No clue. And, yes, that is its only intent," Mike was frustrated, as well. "Listen, I know it doesn't make any sense, but there is no other viable option."

8

Mike phoned Kendra on his way home from meeting with Cat.

"Kendra, it's Mike."

"Hey Mike. Are you driving?"

"Yes."

"Pull over."

"I'll be fine, I'm a smart guy."

"You won't be too smart when you get into an accident. Pull over or I'm hanging up. You're on my clock at the moment."

Mike pulled over into the near Schuster Lake and the Big Thompson River trails. He was still amazed at the destruction caused by the flood just a few years ago.

"Alright, I'm stopped."

"How did things go with Cat?"

"Well, it's weird, actually," Mike sighed.

"Huh, I figured you two would have hit it off pretty well," Kendra chuckled.

"You do like to twist things, don't you? I'm talking about the issue they are seeing with the data."

"Right. What did you two find out?"

"We sent data into Ecolution that they know shows climate change results. Then made a request to pull out the data. The data came back out as Cat called it normalized—all the original temperature readings had been modified, lowered I mean, by a couple of degrees each. Running that data through the model gives non-climate change results. Running the original data through the model gives results consistent with climate change. We then re-ran their unit tests against the original data and was unmodified. It's not their data filter that is modifying the data."

"Huh."

"Yeah. Are you thinking what I'm thinking?" Mike asked.

"Unfortunately, yes. I'll talk to Gil and see if there's any way to get the source for the security filter. It may raise a bit of a stink but that's alright, we need to figure this out. I'll say our penetration testing vendor needs it for full coverage."

"Thanks, Kendra. I'll be back in the office in about an hour. Would have been sooner, but, ya know, someone made me pull over."

"Yeah, well, at least you have a better chance of making it here now. Drive safely. I should have an answer for you by the time you get in."

9

Kendra immediately phoned Gil as soon as she hung up.

"Gil, it's Kendra."

"Hi Kendra. What can I do for you?"

"The security vendor that is performing the penetration testing for the next release is asking for the source code for the security module. Can we get access to it?"

"Why do they need the full source?" Gil asked.

"They want to make sure that if any cryptography is being used, that it's being used properly. A vulnerability in that area of the code has high potential impact," Kendra pushed.

"Would the compiled module be good enough?"

"No, they need to be able to read the source to see the actual implementation," Kendra replied. She was getting the feeling this may be going nowhere.

"Richard tends to be fairly protective of his code and I don't entirely blame him. It could be pretty bad if it got in the wrong hands and was made public."

"True, but if it goes without review and un-tested, it's as good as broken. You know this, because you're a government entity, your site is eventually going to be bombarded with attacks. And they'll find whatever might be open or weak."

"Yep, understood. I'll walk down and talk to Richard now."

"Thanks, Gil."

10

Richard was sitting at his desk typing away on his favorite emacs console when Gil knocked on his office door. Most of his other colleagues left their doors open and welcomed anyone who stopped by. Not Richard. If he could manage it, he would spend all day with his door closed writing code.

"Come in!" he shouted after the knock.

Gil opened the door and walked in. He neither sat down nor asked if Richard had a minute. Richard was likely to say no, and Gil wasn't feeling like being nice or staying long.

"Evolve is preparing for an end-to-end penetration test and needs access to the security module source code," Gil began.

"Not necessary," said Richard.

"Ok, why?"

"We've already had the module tested and the source code reviewed. There were a couple of minor vulnerabilities found and they've been fixed," Richard responded.

"When was that done? I don't remember seeing another team in here or approve a statement of work for it."

"The vendor we worked with was remote. They didn't need to come in. Don't know why you don't remember the statement of work."

"Huh, ok. What was the name of the vendor?" Gil said as he stood to leave.

"Uh, I don't recall off hand."

"When you do remember let me know please," Gil wasn't expecting an answer. He was already out the door.

11

Richard grabbed his phone off his desk as the door was closing behind Gil. He used his fingerprint to unlock the phone and immediately opened Wrapt and hit Jack's username—theboss438.

Gil's poking around asking for source code.

What did you tell him?

Go fuck himself

Why was he asking for it?

Said Evolve needs it for a security audit

Ok, and what did you really tell him, smartass?

Told him we already had a security audit.

What the hell? He approves that shit. He's probably at his desk checking his outbox for approvals he sent.

Fuck. I suppose we'll have to work with that. Did you give him a name of a company?

No

> Good. If he comes around again...actually, do this now...tell him it was Percival Security you worked with. I'll take care of the rest.

A friend of Jack's from college owned Percival Security, David Egan. Jack owed David a favor for helping him out after his miserable marriage fell apart. This was Jack's chance to pay David back and solve his own problem. Jack walked down to one of his favorite empty offices, walked in and locked the door behind him. He then dialed David's cell.

"David, it's Jack."

"Hey buddy, how are you?"

"Good. Hey, I'm going to throw a small amount of money your way and I need you to send me signed copies of a statement of work, non-disclosure, and master services agreement—all backdated two months."

"Sounds great. When do you need the actual work done and what exactly is it for? Who should we talk to for scope?

"No need for any of that. Just put together a generic statement of work."

"I like the sound of that."

"And if anyone happens to come around asking about it, tell them your team worked on a project out of the Fort Collins USDA NITC office with a Richard Knight."

"Works for me."

Jack hung up and walked back to his office. He opened his laptop and logged into the USDA's procurement application. He spent a few minutes entering in some bogus information about the mythical contract with Percival Security, attached the statement of work and other documents David emailed him in the meantime, and topped it off with an approval from Gil.

Picking his phone back up, he re-opened Wrapt and scrolled down to MisterWint.

Scare the crap out of her. She needs to be shown a clear path to two alternatives. Either give up looking for problems or give up the software altogether.

Done.

Done like done-done or done like last time?

He got no response and didn't care to wait for one. He just wanted it taken care of. Jack then flipped back to his email and began writing a memo to his staff.

12

Gil called Kendra back a few short minutes after leaving Richard's office.

"It's Gil. Oddly, Richard claims that another security vendor already tested and reviewed the filter. All vulnerabilities were remediated and verified. I don't remember ever approving a statement of work for this, but bigger items have gotten past me before. And, er...," Gil fell silent and several seconds passed.

"Still there, Gil?" Kendra asked.

"Yeah, one sec, reading through an email I just received from Jack Denning. Seems to be related," Gil said at almost a whisper.

Kendra waited.

"Jack says that none of the security team's code is to be released to anyone outside the team, even within the Department. It's a matter of security and there are no exceptions. That's eerily coincidental," Gil trailed off once again.

"What about just the compiled module itself then?"

"Sorry, no. He includes that in his list of restricted items, as well. Sorry, Kendra, I wish I could help you. Jack's directive ties my hands on this one. But, if what Richard says is true, it's already been tested."

"Alright, thanks anyway Gil."

Kendra hit the hang up button and sat there looking out her office window onto the Pearl Street pedestrian mall. Mike was walking hurriedly across it toward the building entrance.

13

Kendra was standing at her office door when Mike walked through the entrance.

"No luck," she said dryly. "Come, let's whiteboard this out. There's got to be a way of figuring this out."

Kendra walked to her whiteboard and started drawing out the whole platform including the integration points, the security module and all the filters, models and other integration points Nikolaj's team's data was passing through. Then she diagramed out the data flow and how it changed through the system.

"Anything I missed, Mike?" she asked.

"As usual, no," Mike sagged back in the chair he was sitting in.

"Then the only other possibility is that there is another filter intercepting the data and modifying it," Kendra said matter-of-factly.

"And that's not the case either. I called James to confirm there were no other modules deployed in that integration point." James Powers was the Systems Administrator responsible for maintaining the production system that Ecolution ran on along with Ecolution itself.

"That leaves no other option besides the security module," said Kendra.

"Correct."

"Mike, go grab Katie and bring me James' number when you come back."

Mike slid out of his chair still deep in thought. Two minutes later he came back with Katie. Katie was the security expert on the team and was familiar with what Richard and his team implemented. She had implemented libraries like it many times and was deeply familiar with what was involved. "I filled her in on what we're trying to figure out," Mike said.

"Great. Please get James on the phone. Put him on speaker," Kendra said. Ten seconds later they heard the ringtone and seconds after that James picked up.

"This is James."

"Hi James, this is Kendra at Evolve with Mike and Katie on speaker. We were wondering if you could help us out. We're troubleshooting an issue for one of the teams."

"Oh, right, Mike and I were just talking about that. What other info do you need?" James asked.

"Would you please list off all the plugins in the first global and data filter integration plugins directory along with their sizes?" Kendra asked.

"File sizes? Why do you need that? Just curious," James asked, slightly confused.

"We just want to make sure we're working with the correct plugin versions," Kendra lied.

James listed the few plugin files that were in that directory but left out the security plugin.

"James, are there any other plugins, such as the security filter or other global plugins?"

"Yeah, just the security plugin. It's just over three megabytes," James said flatly.

Kendra, Mike, and Katie's mouths dropped open. They knew exactly what that meant. Kendra quickly recovered.

"That gives us what we need. Thanks for the help, James." Kendra said.

"Anything else I can do for you?" James said eagerly.

"No, that should do for now. We'll give you a call if we need anything more. Talk to you later." Kendra hung up the phone.

Katie laughed. "Either that team can't write code worth a shit or that plugin does way more than just authenticate and authorize requests!"

"I suspect it's the latter. As much as we have personal issues with Richard, he is not a hack coder. He knows what he's doing.

"That's as much as we're going to get done today. Thanks for the help you two. Mike, if you talk to Cat, let her know we're working on a solution. I don't know what that is at the moment, but I'm working on it. Whatever it may be, it's not going to be a technical one."

Kendra knew this was going to be a sensitive subject to bring up with Gil. She wasn't even sure if he was the one in which to raise it or how. If she had a closer relationship with Dr. Elizabeth Harrison, the Director of the Office of Science Quality and Integrity for the USGS, she would give her a call.

14

Kendra hadn't seen Bandshell Man or the Other Guy in well over a week. She settled on the whole situation having been a mistake. *They were looking for someone else,* she convinced herself, *and mistook me for that person.* She was glad to return to her walks to and from work. They gave her a chance to prepare for and reflect on work. Right now, she had plenty to think through as she was walking Pearl Street on her way home.

Richard was a problem for Gil from day-one. But for whatever reason, Gil put up with it. From a technical standpoint Kendra saw the value Richard provided and knew few engineers as good as he was. But it was also as clear as a freshly washed pane of glass that Richard caused no end of disruption. She appreciated the disruption some of her own engineers caused, but there was a crucial difference—her team questioned each other to make themselves better; Richard questioned to provoke and prove that he was right.

She saw the door to her left open, but it didn't register until it was too late that it sprung open as if from an explosion. A hand wrapped around her mouth and a blindfold over her eyes. Another arm went around her waist from behind and she felt her body rise off the ground. In less than a second, she saw the light go dark behind the blindfold and knew she must be moving down the corridor the door was for. *Someone must have seen that,* she thought.

She felt herself ascend a flight of stairs, a jog to the right, through a door, and down another long hall. From the footsteps, it sounded like there were at least two of them. She tried to scream several times, but nothing came out. The man's arm was now around her chest and she could barely breath. She felt like she was wrapped in tree trunks. Her arms and legs had been bound in what seemed like one fluid motion, along with tape around both her mouth and nose. If they didn't take that off soon, she was going to pass out.

They stopped momentarily, and she heard a beep and a door unlock and open. She felt movement again as she assumed they went through the door. She was forcefully thrust into a cold metal chair and she heard the chair legs screech across the floor. In the same fluid motion as before, her legs and arms were bound to the chair, and the tape from her mouth and the blindfold was yanked off, pulling some of her hair off with it.

Although she had no doubt who these two were, Kendra whirled around to verify. She couldn't tell if the room was pitch black or her eyes were still adjusting to the relief in pressure of the blindfold. Either way she couldn't see anything but heard a door close directly behind her. Then, nothing but silence.

After a minute she realized it was that the room was completely dark. Her hands and feet were starting to tingle from the circulation being cut off. She tried several times to reach up to rub her face where the tape had been covering her mouth, but realized she was fully bound. After a few more minutes, panic began to set in and her breathing became labored. She was shocked out of it by an electronic voice.

"Kendra Williams. You care deeply about your company and about all those who work for you. You care deeply about Nikolaj Mikkelsen. You care deeply about your parents, currently living at 5316 Waverly Court in Tucson, Arizona. And, you care about your dog, Coda. We're going to give you two options. You will choose one of them or the things and people you care deeply about will start running into problems."

"Fuck you." Kendra didn't scream it and she didn't mutter it under her breath. She said it as matter-of-factly as if having a regular conversation. She had been threatened before, though not to this degree. Instead of enhancing her panic, the panic subsided. She knew that if someone was threatening you, it meant that *they* had lost power, not you. *She* was now in control, though obviously not in any physical sense.

"I don't think you're in any position to speak that way, Miss Williams." Her head snapped hard to the right and her left cheek stung. She let out an involuntary cry, tasted iron, and tears welled up in her eyes. Although she still couldn't see what was in the room, she now knew someone else was in it with her.

"Miss Williams, your choices are simple. Either give up the search for the bug in your software—"

"There is no bug in our software. Someone is hacking it."

"Believe what you want. Either give up the search or shut down the software altogether."

"You've mistaken me for someone with the brain of an adolescent. I have more than two choices."

"Again, Kendra, believe what you want. But do remember that if you indeed care about your company, parents, husband, and dog, you will choose a more appropriate route."

She knew the consequences but couldn't stop herself. "And again, douche bag, fuck you!" This time she did yell it. She felt the impact of a fist on the right side of her head this time, but only momentarily before her world faded away.

15

Kendra opened her eyes. She saw the stack of books she left on the coffee table on her back screened-in porch and felt the battered old couch against her right arm and face. Coda lay next to her licking her face. The right side of her face felt like it had met the side of a concrete pillar; the left side not as bad, more like a squash paddle struck it. Her wrists and ankles burned.

A Dobrinka Tabakova piece was playing on her smart speaker. *Jesus,* she thought, *they know way too much about me.* She heard Nikolaj's car drive up and park in the side drive, then heard the front door slam as he came in.

"Alexa off," she said. "Out here, Niki." The words came out of her mouth, but they didn't sound like her. It hurt to talk.

"Hey hon, how was your day?" Nikolaj said before he came through the door. He soon saw her face and his own dropped. "Oh, my, god."

"You like my new look?" Her voice still surprised her.

"What happened?" Nikolaj pulled Kendra to him as he sunk back into the old sofa.

"My friends Bandshell Man and Other Guy finally caught up with me—or so I presume. I never actually saw them, and they used some sort of electronic voice modulator to mask one of their voices."

"Have you called the police?"

"No, I just came to. And, honestly, Nikolaj, I doubt they can or will do anything about it."

"Why not?"

"We discovered something today. Something truly subversive. I think these guys are trying to stop us from finding the truth. We believe someone is hacking Ecolution to purposefully water-down analysis results. This isn't a bug in the software, it's an attack. Unless we stop investigating or kill the project altogether, they threatened us.

"They obviously know where we live—they must have dumped me here after I blacked out."

"You blacked out?"

"I guess I did, but I'll get to that in a minute. They know about you, Coda, and they gave the address of my parents' house. They didn't say exactly what they would do, but given what they did to me, they didn't have to. Nikolaj, I'm scared."

"No kidding."

"I don't know what to do anymore. I feel like someone picked up the earth, shook it around like a snow globe, and now everything is inside-out and upside-down. Our world has abruptly changed. It's not the world we grew up in or the world we knew a couple of years ago. All the rules have been changed on us. The rules are no longer logical—like they changed the laws of physics. People are now being punished for doing the right thing."

Nikolaj stared out past their backyard. He could only sigh. It had taken him over a decade to understand the U.S. and its politics. Now it made no sense to him.

"Let me go get you some water and you can tell me everything from the beginning," he said as he got up slowly, making sure he didn't hurt her. "Go ahead, I'm listening. This related to Mike thinking the problem is in the security module?"

"Precisely."

"But, why—how—that doesn't even make sense?" Nikolaj came back through the door with a glass of water and handed it to Kendra. He began pacing.

"I know, right? It doesn't at all. But every piece of information we've collected is pointing in that direction. After Mike left your office, I called Gil to get the source code for the security module."

"Right, that would tell you right away."

"Exactly. But Richard won't cough it up and minutes after Gil asked him for it, Gil got an email from his boss saying that that code is off limits to anyone besides Richard's team."

"Sorta makes sense."

"Right, but right then? Right after Gil spoke with Richard about it. Seems a bit fishy."

"Fair."

"Then we called one of the IT guys there and asked for a few bits of information such as file sizes for the plugins configured for the initial data filters. The security plugin is about four times the size that an equivalent security module would be—meaning there is a whole lot of code in there that may be doing other things."

"And you suspect that extra code is causing the data anomalies we're seeing? Why would anyone ever do that?"

"Nikolaj, I love you. But sometimes you are much too trusting of human nature. Richard is a complete asshole. I won't claim to understand him or his motives. He is also an extremely intelligent engineer—much more capable than what he's responsible for in that office. Those two attributes are a bad combination."

"I admit to that."

"I still can't prove that the problem is with the security module or Richard's responsible for it. But there's smoke coming from both areas and now I'm getting attacked and threatened."

"Let's go back to that. What did those guys say?"

"They weren't concrete at all. They knew all the things and people I cared about and basically said that if I didn't stop investigating the problem or abandon the software, the people I care about will start running into problems. They didn't say what those problems would be."

"If I know your parents at all, they're going to say the same thing I'm about to say. Don't worry about me. Do what you feel is right. I'll take Coda up to work with me tomorrow and see if Cat will take him for a couple of weeks until this blows over."

"Thanks, hon. I'm not sure if doing the right thing is enough this time, but I'll do it anyway. I honestly don't know what else to do."

"Now let's call the police. This is too big for them to not do something about. If this is as connected to D.C. as you think, maybe they can get the FBI involved."

Investigation

"Mike, it's Kendra," Kendra began.

"Uh, what?" said Mike.

"Listen, I know it's early on a Saturday, but I need to talk out a couple of ideas and for you to start thinking about something for me."

"Oh?"

"I've been thinking about how to inconclusively prove that the security module is modifying the data."

"Don't you ever take a break? And didn't we already prove that?"

"All the weekend is for me is a time to actually think about work. There's never much time *during* work to truly think about it. And, yes, we proved it with circumstantial evidence. But that's not going to be enough when I take this to Gil—it's got to be water tight."

"Ok, so what do you have for me?"

"Two things. First, we need to make sure we're logging the state of the data both before and after it runs through a plugin. That logging needs to be sent directly to the Evolve logging servers and not configurable—no one should be able to turn that off. It also should not be logged to the server logs. I don't want to raise suspicion."

"With you so far."

"Second, and this dovetails with the logging, you know how you implemented the data deserialization component—how the data coming from web requests gets deserialized from the body of the request into data wrapper objects. I want the auditing of those objects to capture the module name and the stack trace anytime the object's data value is changed. The auditing needs to include the entire trail—not just the first or last change, but all of them."

"Sure, that's easy enough through the diagnostics and reflection libraries. We'll just save it to an array."

"And, please be sure to protect those classes. I don't want anyone to be able to override that behavior and remove the auditing."

"Sure enough, boss. Sounds fun, I'm on it now!"

"Last thing. Can you get this done and tested by Wednesday, so it can go out in the next release?"

"Already halfway there—at least the development part. I just need to finish writing some automated tests and I'll have Peter test it this afternoon. Still need to write some tests for it."

"Jesus, Mike. Were you even listening to me?"

"Of course, got it all. Do you need me to repeat it back to you?"

"No need. I shouldn't be surprised at this point. It's still a bit shocking when you go from half asleep to finishing an implementation that would take the average developer two days, in the span of two minutes *while we're talking about it.*"

"It's easier for me to think in code."

"Yeah, got that, Cyborg Mike. Or should I call you Data?"

"Fine by me. But you do know that Data wasn't a cyborg. He was an AI in a totally synthetic body. Now I miss my family on Omicron Theta."

"Wow, just...wow. Between you and Nikolaj, I feel like Bob Dylan with a minor twist—instead of clowns and jokers, I have nerds and geeks on either side of me."

"Nerds to the left of me, geeks to the right. Here I am stuck in the middle with you."

"Not a *bad* voice, but please stick to your day job. We need you here anyway."

"Fair."

"One last thing. Don't bother Peter on the weekend. The last thing I want to do is burn you guys out. Apologies for calling you early on a weekend. I just needed to talk this out."

"Glad you did, and I totally don't mind. Peter won't mind either. We were going to meet to bike up Highway 36 later today anyway. This will be more fun."

"And safer. Never understood the attraction to riding a bike along a narrow highway with only a thin piece of Styrofoam protecting your money maker. But, I digress. Thanks Mike, see you in the office tomorrow."

"Later."

2

Mike spent the next hour writing his automated tests, pushing up his code, creating a code review, and making sure all the continuous integration builds succeeded. He then chatted with Peter to get him up to speed on group chat, so everyone else could also read the conversation and get up to speed later. Peter had Mike's changes downloaded and built on the virtual machine he used for testing, and had the changes thoroughly tested in forty-five minutes.

They finished with plenty of time for a ride up Highway 36 and a couple of beers at Da Beirhaus.

3

Richard sat at his computer watching several windows on his three monitors. He possessed no trust in the Evolve team. *Not that they were smart enough to figure out his algorithms or what he had even done,* he thought. But they had been snooping around and he was taking no chances.

One of his windows showed the web traffic going through the security proxy he set up. The proxy filtered all traffic coming in and out of the USDA infrastructure. Certain traffic, such as to and from the Evolve domain, and any other domains he found registered to the company, were immediately paused so that he could examine the request before it could pass through. All requests *to* those domains were immediately killed. He didn't need to know the content of the requests—there was no reason for those to occur as far as he was concerned.

Another window showed the various log files, updated in real time. He wanted to know what was being logged and make sure there wasn't any unnecessary information. This was best practice for a production system anyway—only log what you need so you don't slow the system.

The last window was a custom application he created which monitored the data coming into the security module and the resulting data coming out of it. He wanted to make sure the data was being modified properly.

He was monitoring all these items to make sure nothing went awry when Evolve updated Ecolution today—that Evolve didn't ruin his work, or his future. There was big money in this, at least for him. If he kept this going for the next three years—until President Holloway's second term was over—he'd walk away with five-hundred thousand dollars. With what he'd already saved for retirement, he could do just that.

Richard had never had much money, especially as a kid. This was his chance to break away. He had grown up not far from Fort Collins in the town of Greeley. He was an only child of a single mom. His dad worked the oil rigs and the family had moved to various places throughout the country until his mom got fed up with the moving and the womanizing by her husband. His mom left his dad when Richard was eight. His dad didn't seem to care much—he didn't spend much time at home anyway. Life wouldn't change much for him. He wouldn't get to see his son, Richard, as much—but then again, he didn't have much of a connection with him. Richard didn't mind either. He barely knew the man. His dad wasn't so much "dad" to him, as that guy who stopped in occasionally, to sleep over.

Money was always tight for them. Richard grew up on everyone else's hand-me-downs. He didn't mind though, they were just cloths. There were many more important things, like the mental challenge of school—for a while anyway. By the end of his fourth-grade year. Around that time his mother managed scrounge enough money to purchase a Commodore VIC-20 on her meager salary as a secretary at the University of Northern Colorado Department of Mathematics. Richard was ten.

Richard spent hours after school writing programs in Commodore's version of BASIC. Although you couldn't do much with BASIC, Richard was able to create elaborate choose your own adventure type games. He didn't end up playing them much but enjoyed the process of writing the code that made it all possible. He loved creating. Unfortunately, he didn't have many friends to share his creations with. He couldn't help himself telling others when they were wrong. Most people don't like being told they're wrong. Richard never grasped why. If he was wrong about something, he'd want to know—why don't they?

He quickly became bored with the VIC-20 and graduated onto the IBM XT which he borrowed time on from a mathematics professor in the department his mother worked. The IBM had a floppy drive which Richard thought was a vast improvement from the Commodore's cassette tape storage. He couldn't really do much more with IBM BASIC, but the color screen was certainly an improvement.

As the University upgraded computers, Richard reaped the rewards and his creations became more advanced—until he discovered that you could also *destroy* things with code. After leaving several floppies containing a boot program that wiped the computer's system in drives throughout the mathematics department, Richard was banned from the department. His mother was also let go from her job.

In 1989 Richard started college at Colorado State University working toward a degree in computer science. With his penchant for telling people they were wrong, he quickly angered all of his professors. It made for a long four years—not so much for him, but for his TA's and professors.

"Professor Kargard, you know if you use a quicksort there instead of a merge sort it would be almost three times faster", Richard interrupted in his Introduction to Algorithms class.

"Ehem, yes, of course I know that. That's not the point of this lecture, though", Dr. Kargard said.

"Why would you teach us to use a less efficient algorithm in this situation? It's just plain wrong."

Toward the end of his time at CSU he met Gil Whittaker, who though he worked as a scientist for the USDA spent a lot of time in the Warner School of Natural Resources. Gil had been looking for a brilliant technical resource to build computer models for his work. Gil often attended the Software Engineering seminars to see what some of the students were like, who asked questions, and how insightful those questions were.

One evening in the spring of Richard's senior year, they both attended the seminar, "Improving Software Development Productivity with CASE Tools." Computer aided software engineering tools were becoming all the rage at the time and many people, like the poor graduate student giving the seminar, were sold. The graduate student kept driving home that the tool he was working to develop as part of his thesis, would improve productivity by ten-fold. Richard didn't wait for the end to ask questions, nor did he even have a question. He stood up and bellowed,

"Have you not read Fred Brooks' *No Silver Bullet* article? Hurray for trying but let's get real. You keep saying over and over that teams will see a ten-fold productivity increase by using this tool. Brooks explained well that you're not going to see that. You want to improve productivity, then hire a great programmer—clearly not you."

Disgusted, Richard walked out of the room and Gil slipped out behind him.

"Hey, nice little speech there. I guess you weren't terribly impressed with his tools", Gil said as he came up behind Richard.

"Not at all," Richard said as he turned around to see who was talking to him. "And did you see his data analysis that supposedly showed his productivity increase? That was a disgusting use of statistics. Who let that guy into grad school anyway?"

"Do you have a background in math and science, too?", asked Gil.

"Yeah, more than that guy anyway. But that could be done by waking up in the morning."

Though clearly rough around the edges, Richard fit the bill. *Actually*, Gil thought, *he might fit right in with some of the other arrogant scientists.*

After graduation Richard began working for Gil at the USDA. However, because of his lack of a PhD and lack of a background in ecology, he found it difficult to gain the respect from the scientists he worked with. He didn't seem to mind in the least. He was happy enough diving into the complexity of the models Gil and others asked him to build—and pointing out when they were wrong about something.

Richard's computer skills attracted the attention of Gil's managers and eventually all the way up to Jack Denning, the Deputy Director of Research and Development for the Forest Service. Denning recognized the need for a formal team in charge of information system security and was looking for someone to lead this team. It fit perfectly that Richard already worked at the USDA National Information Technology Center.

Richard took to his new position like a duck to water. He couldn't believe that he was now *allowed* to try to break things, test limits, and show others their technical limitations and problems. Richard excelled at his new job. Jack continued to take notice.

As Evolve Inc began the implementation of the new Ecolution software infrastructure that promised to revolutionize science in government, Jack Denning tasked Richard with a new initiative. One that no one else was to know about—ever.

Kendra had been right—Richard didn't need to spend a lot of time on the security authorization module. That was easy. He spent most of his time on a data filter hidden away within the security module that pushed data values back to historic norms. During the Ecolution initiative, the USGS and USDA also began pooling all their historic climate and land use data into the same databases that would house the new data inputs, as well.

It was complicated to pull the right historic values given the disparate nature of all the data the two agencies had collected over past 100 plus years of existence. Temperature values could be measured in Celsius or Fahrenheit, for example. He even found a group measuring temperature in Kelvin. And temperature norms varied greatly by area and elevation—even having normal variation between years and decades. That was only one variable among dozens, maybe hundreds. But it was a challenge Richard enjoyed and excelled at.

The normal activity in his three windows slowed to a trickle and then died out altogether. They must have shut everything down in preparation for the upgrade. It would likely take them fifteen to twenty minutes to perform the upgrade and restart the services. There was time for a quick break.

He headed down the hallway toward the restroom. He turned the corner and saw Peter from Evolve headed toward him. *Jeez, not this dweeb again—got another joke for me, you jerk*, Richard thought to himself.

"Hey Richard, how's it goin'? Keeping the government's data safe from all the crazy farmers out there?" Peter joked.

Richard didn't bother responding. *If you don't have anything intelligent to say, shut your damn hole.* He passed Peter with no expression at all. Peter wasn't totally surprised, but it still irked him that Richard couldn't bother himself to even acknowledge him. *Jesus, you weird, evil robot*, thought Peter.

Richard finished his business, grabbed a cup of the awful, sludge coffee they made in the kitchen and headed back to his desk. His windows still showed no signs of life.

A few minutes past, then he saw the startup messages appear in the logs. A couple of minutes later, he saw the message:

```
Starting Ecolution 3.1 at 11:04 MST
Listening on port 9443
```

Alright, so they had enough brains to get the software back up and running. Goddamn miracle. A couple more messages came up in the logs. They must be running a smoke test to make sure things were running as expected. Then he saw some activity coming through from the security module. Nothing changed there— the data looked like it was modified as he needed.

A paused request to one of the Evolve domains popped up in his proxy window. He opened the request details to see what they were attempting to send themselves. Probably some usage data, but usage data they will never see.

What the hell, this isn't usage data! He saw the stack traces they were sending back. He saw the stack traces with references to his security module. And he saw the audit trail that showed exactly how his code was changing data values. *Holy shit,* he thought. *This is not good.*

He looked at a couple more of the requests. More and more of them sending back the same data. He turned off the breakpoint that paused the requests and let them all be killed by his filter. He slammed his coffee cup down and swore as his coffee splashed all over his desk and keyboard.

Assholes!

4

"Now it's my turn for a coffee break," said Mike as he spun around in his chair and got up for the door.

"I'll join you," Peter shot out to follow Mike, hoping Jim Powers, the USDA System Administrator, wouldn't want to join them, too.

As soon as they got out of the door, Peter grabbed Mike's elbow. "Mike, somethings up. None of the logging requests to our servers are getting through. I checked the Ecolution logs and the requests are being made, but the logs on our Evolve server show no requests and there's no data in the database. My guess is Dick setup a proxy and is filtering those out. If he did, he's going to know what's up."

Just as Peter finished they both saw Richard rounding the corner, looking like he wanted to kill someone.

"I'm going to venture you're right, Peter," Mike said out of the side of his mouth.

"What the fuck are you guys up to? You know you have no business sending government information out of our network!"

"Woah, what's going on here, Richard? There's no need for that language," Gil said from the other end of the hall.

They were all surprised to hear Gil's voice, but Richard was still so mad he didn't show it.

"These guys are trying to send back data to their servers about proprietary government security implementations in their logging framework. No government data should *ever* leave this network," Richard said.

"Apologies. We were just trying to collect usage data, so we could determine how best to tune the system," Mike replied.

"Bullshit!" Richard said.

"Richard, that's enough—stay professional. Let's take this to the conference room," Gil said.

They walked into the neighboring conference room and Gil closed the door. They all remained standing.

"Richard is correct in that we can't have government security information, or any government information for that matter, sent outside our network. We'll need to turn that off. With that said, is there any other way you could collect the information you need without it leaving our network?" said Gil.

"Good god! They aren't collecting tuning information they're pulling stack traces out of the security module—it's a gigantic security breach! These guys should be fired!" Richard fired back.

"Gil, we're happy to turn that off and revisit how we can collect the information we need in a manner that fits with your policies. We didn't realize it would be a problem. Can I suggest Kendra give you a call to work that out?" Mike said.

"Didn't realize it would be a problem. Right," said Richard.

"That sounds good, Mike. I appreciate the flexibility. And, yes, have Kendra reach out. Mike and Peter, please go take care of that now and let me know when everything is back up and running."

"Thanks, Gil," said Mike.

"This isn't over," said Richard.

"Seems like it's over," Peter muttered just loud enough for Mike to hear.

5

When Mike and Peter returned to James they explained the situation and reconfigured the system. Mike had decided to make it configurable at the last minute in case something like this arose. He still needed the update running.

6

"Shit, that went well," said Peter after they packed up and were headed back to the car. Mike didn't respond until they got back to the car. As soon as the door shut he replied.

"No worries, I also put in a back door to get the same information. A data input request specifically into Nikolaj's team's repository with a debug flag set to true in the request will give us the data. We only need to use it once to get the info we need. Even if Richard spots it, it will likely be too late unless he's sitting their inspecting every request and response before letting it pass and that would be insane."

"Richard is insane," said Peter.

"Yes, but not stupid. He's a smart guy, but he's not the only smart one around here."

7

Richard sat seething in his chair. He didn't like feeling out of control, especially because of a couple of hacks as he saw them. He needed Jack to get these guys off his back and fast.

I think they know.

Who knows what?

I think Evolve knows we're modifying the data.

Why do you think that?

They upgraded the system today. It contains code to capture data changes, log where in the code the change was made, and send that info back to their servers. If it weren't for my proxy, they would have that data in their hands.

I don't know or care what a proxy is, but you're saying they DON'T have the data?

Correct.

Then what are you worried about?

They have access to all other code except the security module. They wouldn't be trying to pull that information if they thought it was something caused by their own code. They must know it's being changed by the security module and are looking to prove it.

They've overspent their welcome as it is and have served their purpose. I think it's time to get rid of them. That shouldn't take me long. In the meantime, continue making sure that information doesn't get out.

You said they were trying to send data outside the USDA network?

Yep

That makes it easy. We can terminate them on breach of contract.

That's what I told them. That it was a security breach anyway.

Good. This should be easy. We can have them surrender the code to the USDA and you can own it from here on out.

8

Instead of heading back to the Boulder office, Mike and Peter drove just up the road to Nikolaj's office to see Cat and Anir. They had to park off the main campus next to the Center for the Arts and School of Music, now housed in the old Fort Collins High School.

"Would you believe I went to high school here?" said Mike.

"There were schools when you were a kid?" said Peter.

"Yes, smart ass. But this underpass wasn't here back then, so if you were taking a college-level class you had to brave crossing College Ave on your own."

They enjoyed the short walk to the SoS building and made their way up the stairs. Mike knocked on Cat's door. She turned around and huge grin grew on her face as she saw Mike. Peter noticed and gave Mike a questioning look, but Mike wasn't looking— he had the same huge grin on his face.

"Hey, Cat. Just thought we'd drop in and say hi. Also have some potential news about the data issue. How are you?" said Mike.

"Well, thanks. And you?" said Cat.

"He's good," Peter interrupted. "I'm here too—doing well, thanks—and Anir is over there, I bet he's doing well too."

"Um, ok. So, what's the news?" asked Cat.

"Mike here is brilliant—as I'm sure you know—and he wrote a little code in Ecolution to tell us what and who is unwelcomingly modifying your data. He is here to show that off—and probably some other things, which I don't really care to see—and swoop in like Prince Valiant and present you with the answer to your deepest question," said Peter.

Both Cat and Mike were visibly embarrassed. Anir was also staring at Peter but was clearly still trying to figure out what Peter was getting at.

"With that, I will turn it over to Mike while I sit over in the corner and let you two make out, I mean, talk," said Peter.

Mike had a deer in the headlights look.

"You updated Ecolution to identify the data issue," said Cat.

"Yeah. We just need to make some of the same requests to the server as we were doing last week, but with one minor change," said Mike.

"Here, you take my seat at the keyboard and work your magic," said Cat.

"Don't Peter. Whatever you're going to say, just don't," said Mike.

"Not even just a little?"

"Not even."

Mike looked back at the monitor. "Let's open up the same request client," Mike's fingers danced through a series of keyboard shortcuts. Soon he had the request client and the notes from last time open in two separate windows. "And copy-paste this in. Just need to add this flag...and send." They waited a little while for the response to return. It did, and Mike scrolled through the long body of the response that contained the stack trace he was looking for.

"Bingo, there it is down to the classes and line numbers. Richard's security module is the culprit, and this is exactly what Kendra needed to take to Gil," said Mike.

"How can you tell? What are you looking at that says that, Mike?" Cat asked.

"See this line here? This line tells us the precise line of code that alters your data, what the original value was, and what it was modified to. Does this original data value look familiar?" said Mike.

"Move over and I'll check," said Cat.

She opened two files side by side.

"This file here is the original dataset we were using to test last week. And this file shows the modified dataset we pulled back out. Looking down through here...yes, here it is. This value is the original and the modified value is this one...which matches the modified value you just showed me in the—what did you call it? —stack trace?" Cat said.

"Yeah, stack trace. Well, technically the original and modified values were a part of this data structure here but doesn't matter. The important part is we see without a doubt that the security module is modifying the code," Mike said.

"What's the excitement about?" Nikolaj interrupted from behind them.

"Good timing, Nikolaj. Should we get Kendra on the speakerphone too?" asked Mike.

"Yeah," Nikolaj said as he stepped forward and dialed Kendra's cell on Cat's phone, putting her on speaker.

"Hey, Cat," Kendra's voice came over the speaker.

"Hey hon, it's Nikolaj, Cat, Anir, Mike and Peter. You're on speaker and they seem to have some news," Nikolaj said.

"We have got the stack trace—not how we originally intended—but we got it. I'll update you on why we had to change gears later. Essentially, it's pointing directly to the security module," said Mike.

"Why would they ever want to modify the data? It doesn't make any sense," Nikolaj said.

"I totally hear ya—no clue," said Mike.

"I'm starting to think this is much bigger than we think it is. I don't know what it is, but I smell a bigger fish in this pond," Kendra said over the speaker.

"But why would anyone want to change our data?" Nikolaj asked.

"That's the right question—who would gain by changing your data? Ecolution was going to make running ecological models exponentially more efficient. Scientists such as you, Nikolaj, would be able to publish more papers faster. And they, whoever this is, don't want those papers to show the results they've been showing. In your case, and in the case of the majority of teams using and intending to use Ecolution, your data has inconclusively been showing results supporting climate change. Whoever is behind this is afraid of the accelerated pace of climate change support," said Kendra.

"That sounds like a giant leap from what we currently know. How can we prove that?" said Nikolaj.

"You may be right. I really don't know. It's only a guess. But at this point, we don't need to prove it. We've proved that some other entity is erroneously changing data inputs. This is enough to bring to Gil and he can figure it out—or get someone involved who can.

"That's a good segue to my earlier point. Gil's expecting a call from you and it may not be a pleasant one. Richard was running a proxy which caught our requests out to the Evolve servers. He saw the data we were trying to pass and through quite a hissy fit. Gil witnessed the whole thing and largely sided with Richard—at least to the extent that we violated USDA policy by trying to send their data outside their network," said Mike.

"I knew that might be a problem and was prepared for that conversation," said Kendra.

"You were ahead of me on that one," said Mike.

"But not ahead on everything. How did you get the stack traces and data structure changes we needed?" asked Kendra.

"I also added it to responses to Nikolaj's team's data repository input requests. By adding a debug flag to the requests, it returns the same data we were trying to post to our servers. But it's only available for Nikolaj's repository. It shouldn't be discoverable by anyone else," said Mike.

"Well done. Way to save our asses. Gil will forget about the data breach once I tell him what we were looking for, why, and what we found," said Kendra.

9

"Hi Kendra, it's Gil Whittaker," Gil started.

"Hey Gil, good to hear from you. Were your ears burning? I was just getting ready to call you," Kendra responded.

Gil chuckled. "Oh, that can't be good. Actually, I'm pretty sure what you were calling about. You spoke with Mike, I presume."

"Ha, it's always good when *you* are the subject. But in this case, it involves something that is potentially unsavory that you might be able to help out with. Mike did tell me about the external network request issue. This is related."

"Good timing. I have something I think you can help me out with, too. Dr. Elizabeth Harrison is in town early next week and would like an update on Ecolution and its adoption. I believe you've already met her at least once in person. Would you be able to come up to the Research Center on Monday of next week and spend the day with us?" Gil asked.

"Absolutely...if you're willing to give me some advice," Kendra said hesitantly.

"Of course. What about?"

"It's a bit of a sensitive subject. I'll just cut to the chase. Various teams who have been early adopters of Ecolution are seeing odd results out of their models that are suddenly inconsistent with climate change trends. The issue appeared to be that something was filtering and normalizing their data to make it appear that climate change is not occurring. We have ruled out any of the other teams' data filter plugins." Kendra gave a long pause.

"Our tests narrowed it down to the authentication plugin that Richard wrote. It appeared to be doing more than just authentication. I know how odd that sounds—and it sounded just as odd to us. This is where the external network requests were coming into play. We needed to prove inconclusively where the data was being modified. I didn't think it would be fair to you to come with circumstantial evidence only.

"This was not Mike's decision, it was mine. I asked him to do it. In addition to the external logging mechanism, he also wired up the data input web service to give us the same information. We ran that yesterday afternoon. It inconclusively shows that the security module, including the precise line of code within that module, is modifying the data." Kendra paused again to wait for Gil to respond, but there was silence.

"Apologies, Gil, we needed a way to figure this out and this was the only way we could do it. If it didn't have such a huge negative impact, we would have taken a different route. But the consequences to this are huge," Kendra continued.

"No, I totally understand. I just gotta process this," Gil finally responded.

"I realize Richard has worked for you for quite some time and this is a highly sensitive thing to accuse someone of, particularly in the current political climate. No pun intended."

Gil responded in his usual manner, put frustrations aside, and pierced through to what mattered. "OK, give me all the facts. What data is being manipulated, what tests have you run to prove this, and who all is affected?"

Kendra took him through all the tests that Nikolaj's team had done along with the tests that Mike had come up with and implemented across several of the teams, along with the details of the stack trace and data structure modifications output. Half way through Gil was completely convinced but let Kendra finish.

"Thanks, Kendra. And nice work. This is why your team was hired in the first place—you're all incredibly smart and thorough.

"I need to think through this a little more, but let's prepare to bring this to Elizabeth on Monday. I arranged for you and me to have a private meeting with her later in the afternoon. She wanted to congratulate you in person. I hate to do this to her, but of anyone, she will know how to handle this delicately and keep Evolve clean of it.

"That said, this may be a bumpy ride. I know it seems like an open and shut case, but my political radar is putting up some bad juju. I can only guess how far up the chain this goes, and it may go all the way."

"However far it goes up the chain, I'd venture to say that they're all aware we're onto them. If Richard saw what was contained in those requests, he knows what we were looking for," said Kendra.

10

Throughout Monday morning, Kendra and Gil accompanied Dr. Harrison, visiting with many of the teams involved in the initial adoption of Ecolution. Kendra knew the nature of these site visits and how they were generally a stage on which the staff made it sound and appear as if everything was dandy. Usually the status of things wasn't just dandy, and no one ever gained from the charade. But government and corporate offices did it every day. *Don't show the boss that something is wrong, because that won't reflect well on our group.* Yeah, well, if someone would give the boss the honest situation, then they'd be able to help make it better. And that's what they did.

All the teams were impressed with the new system and wondering why they hadn't implemented something like it earlier. But, they had concerns and let Dr. Harrison know them. Elizabeth listened patiently and made sure they understood she was on it. She also asked them to keep her and Gil informed as they discovered additional issues. Elizabeth knew these scientists would not keep what they knew under wraps. They weren't the gossip types—they were the let-us-get-this-fixed types.

Gil had warned Elizabeth ahead of time to expect the concerns the scientists would voice and alluded to Kendra's knowledge of the situation. They would fill her in on the details after the team meetings. Once they finished up the last of the meetings, Elizabeth got right down to business.

"Kendra, I understand you have more details on the concerns the teams have been expressing. Lay it out for me in as much detail as you've given Gil. And, I know you probably would anyway, but I need you to be completely honest and blunt with me. I won't be able to help if I don't fully understand the situation."

"Understood," Kendra began. She continued to outline in detail all the steps Nikolaj's team and Mike and the Evolve team had taken to discover the issue and narrow down the source.

"Now, from that last piece of evidence I showed you, we know exactly where that module is modifying the data, and I can definitively prove

Richard wrote it. I just don't know *why* he wrote it." Kendra finished up.

"Thank you, Kendra. Let's take a break for lunch and meet back here in thirty minutes. Gil, I need this room to make a few calls. Would you please pick up a salad for me wherever you go?"

"Absolutely on both counts." Gil answered.

Gil and Kendra left the room, both breathing sighs of relief as they closed the door behind them. Without talking they set out of the building, over the skybridge that spanned the Mason bike trail, train tracks, and transit road, and into the grocery store to grab lunch. They both headed to the sandwich bar and ordered sandwiches—Gil went over to the salad bar while they waited and put together a salad for Elizabeth. Gil was so deep in thought he nearly forgot to pay for their food. They headed back over to the Research Center and entered the conference room where they had left Elizabeth.

"Just in time," she said. "I have Special Agent Jason Wellington on the phone. Jason, this is Kendra Williams from Evolve Inc and Gil Whittaker, from the USDA. Jason specializes in domestic cybercrime and I've known him for years now. Jason and I already discussed what you laid out for me, Kendra. As it turns out, Jason's team was already investigating Richard Knight and the peer of mine you know from the USDA, Jack Denning, because of some suspicious communications between the two of them."

"Yeah, as it turns out, your favorite secure encrypted messenger isn't so secure," Jason joked.

"You mean, like Wrapt?" Kendra knew about encrypted messenger apps but hadn't yet heard that any of the three-letter acronym intelligence agencies had cracked them yet.

"Exactly. Jack Denning's social media behaviour triggered a flag for us over a year ago. Everyone who knows him or knows who he is understands that he's a climate change skeptic. That's no news and it's no crime either. But our text analysis system alerted us to subversive and deceptive text patterns in his tweets. That suggested he may be either planning or doing something not entirely in the up-and-up for his position.

"We began a preliminary fact-finding investigation to see if there was anything to this pattern and there were more signs as we dug in. According to some folks who worked in and around his office, he had been having secretive meetings with Richard Knight, stepping into empty offices to take phone calls, and other such suspicious behaviour.

"That's when we started actively monitoring his emails, phone calls, and other communications. He seems to be fairly careful overall. His stepping into empty offices to take phone calls must have stopped before our monitoring started. But at some point, he started using an encrypted messenger app—the one you mentioned Ms. Williams—and that's when we learned about Richard Knight and the work he was doing on Ecolution. We didn't know the name of the software or many of the other details you shared with Dr. Harrison until now. But it all matches up.

"Richard Knight's psychological profile also matches with someone who would commit such a crime. Mr. Knight actually applied for an internship with the Bureau out of college, before he started with the USDA. He was rejected for this very reason—he matched the profile of someone who might use his computer skills to subvert the government or other large enterprise, just for the fun of it. According to the records collected when he applied, he wrote a simple boot program that wiped several of the new computers in the Department of Mathematics at the University of Northern Colorado back in the mid-80's. That seems to have been a precursor to his current work. He is clearly an intelligent guy but seems to have trouble directing his skills for good."

"We'd always known he was a pain in the ass to work with, but didn't realize he would become a criminal," Kendra replied with almost a sigh.

"I think you captured it well, Ms. Williams, he is a criminal. A lot of folks might brush this off as a minor hacking, but it's full-scale computer fraud. If I understand the implications that Dr. Harrison described to me, the effects of these changes could change government policy related to climate change."

"That's exactly right, Jason," Elizabeth interjected. "The reports that guide those types of policies are effectively compilations of the conclusions of analyses done by many of the scientists in my and Jack's agencies. Obviously, Jack knows this, and although he and others of his persuasion are simultaneously intimidating and censoring climate scientists, it appears he thought he could just bend the data itself to match his beliefs."

Gil followed the entire discussion and was appalled and felt somewhat responsible for what had happened—he had hired Richard after all. He was looking for someone who thought differently, and he got it. "Ok, so Elizabeth, Jason, what are our next steps?"

"I'll let Jason take that one," Elizabeth answered.

"First thing is that I need to take this to my boss. If it were only Mr. Knight, this would be easy to handle. With the involvement of Dr. Denning as a Deputy Director, this will need to be handled with finesse."

"Jason?" Kendra interrupted.

"Yeah?"

"There's one more thing."

"Shoot."

"You just mentioned intimidation." She hesitated. Kendra didn't want to bring it up but now felt is needed to be said. "I was attacked and threatened late last week by two men who gave me an ultimatum. They told me to drop investigating this issue or they would hurt the people closest to me."

Both Gil and Elizabeth looked straight at Kendra, surprised and sympathetic.

"We know that too, Kendra. I'm sorry you had to go through that. I admit we were behind the eight-ball on that one. Those two were ex-military special forces who joined the dark side. They were essentially muscle for hire. We had been monitoring them but hadn't made the connection yet between the services they were offering and Jack's activity. They have since been removed from the equation. Please accept my sincerest apologies."

"Will there be more?"

"I'd be lying if I said, 'no'. But I will say we're keeping a closer eye on it. I know it doesn't always feel this way, but the local police got your back, too."

She gave him an uneasy smile. Jason nodded back in understanding.

11

The following day as Kendra sat at her desk, she felt relief that the issue was now in the FBI's hands. She was finishing up her first cup of coffee of the day when her phone rang. The area code on the caller ID read 202. *Washington D.C.*, she thought. *Must be a follow-up from the FBI.*

Kendra picked up the phone. "Evolve. This is Kendra."

"Jack Denning. I hear there was a security breach."

Kendra knew what he was referring to but waited for an explanation. The tone of his voice suggested he was after more than simply to give

Kendra a slap on the wrist. The last thing she wanted to do was directly admit to him that they knowingly broke their contract.

"A security breach caused by your software. A deliberately constructed component that passed— sorry, attempted to pass— government information out to your own servers."

"And you're burying—sorry, attempting to bury—the truth."

Jack laughed. "You will be burying your business and possibly your entire career if you're not careful."

Kendra's face burned, and she gritted her teeth, but she knew she needed to keep her cool.

"I'll give you a couple of options," said Jack. "We can terminate this contract immediately, leaving your company without work—and, as I understand it, you in financial ruin."

"You have no idea what my finances look like."

"Or you keep your mouths shut, ignore what you found, and drop it." He paused. "And, yes, I have your account balances right here. Would you like me to read them off?"

How can he possibly have my bank account balances? she thought.

"I also have Nikolaj's accounts—looks like his retirement will be postponed indefinitely. Would you like to keep your company afloat or be right?"

"Which option, Ms. Williams?"

12

Kendra sat looking out the window of her office, playing with her fidget cube, and thinking. *If this is game time, what's my next play,* she thought. *This is bigger than just me, it's bigger than Evolve and the USDA. There are people all around the country struggling with this. But I desperately need that money.*

Just then her phone rang. The area code was Denver or Boulder, but the number didn't look familiar.

"Evolve Incorporated, this is Kendra," she said.

"Hi Kendra. Special Agent Wellington," the voice on the other end of the line said.

"Oh, hi, Jason. What can I do for you?" she answered.

"Nothing. I just wanted to let you know that we're not letting you hang out to dry."

"Sorry, Jason. What do you mean?"

"We're aware that the USDA is threatening to dissolve your contract."

"How could you possibly know about that?"

"Uh." Pregnant silence. *Jason needs work on his secret-keeping,* Kendra thought.

"So, I spoke with my boss yesterday after we spoke with you, Elizabeth, and Gil," he continued.

"And you're not going to tell me how you know about the threat are you?"

"My boss gave me and my team the go-ahead to pursue Jack, Richard, and whomever else is involved. Though as we guessed, he asked me to do so with care."

"Good. Where does that leave me and my company? Is there anything you need me to do?"

"No. Nor can I promise that Evolve will ever see that contract again. I just couldn't bear to let you feel your efforts were for nothing."

"Thanks, Jason. I do appreciate that you're pursuing this. If nothing else, for anyone else who may be affected. And just for the sake that it's not right."

Kendra hung up the phone and hung her head. Keep going, she thought to herself. Just keep going. She then headed home, not knowing how or what she was going to do to keep going.

13

Kendra sat at her desk overlooking the walking mall, sipping on her second coffee of the morning. Out of the corner of her eye, she saw Jacqui peek in the door.

"Good morning, Kendra. Ready to talk yet?", Jacqui said.

"How did you know we needed to talk?"

"You look exhausted. More than usual. Did you sleep at all last night?"

"No."

"Gil also called last night after you left and filled me in on Jack's ultimatum."

"Asshole. Not Gil."

"I know." Jacqui paused. "Don't take it. Whatever Jack offered you as an out, don't take it. Gil didn't know the specifics and I don't want to know either. But whatever it is, it's not worth compromising with that scumbag."

"If I refuse we're done, Jacqui. We have nothing left in reserves."

"Then we're done."

Kendra sighed.

"I can't let you down like that. I can't let the company we've built down. We've worked so hard and come so far. This contract was setting us up for other bigger contracts down the road."

"So, what? It's not like you and I can't find something different. And all those people out there, we hired every one of them. We know they're good at what they do. That's why we hired them. They'll have no problems finding new gigs. Half of them can roll out of bed in the morning into their next jobs without trying."

Kendra and Jacqui both stared out on the growing numbers walking the mall on their way to work.

"Kendra?"

"Yeah." Kendra knew what she needed to do.

"After you call Jack we can sit down and figure out our transition plan."

Jacqui gave her a smile and walked out. Picking up the phone, Kendra dialed Jack's number.

"Made your decision, Kendra? Success and happiness or burn your business to the ground?"

"Truth is what I chose."

14

After three hours of working through transition scenarios, Kendra was ready to go home. But she knew she had to do one more thing before the day was done. Both she and Jacqui cared deeply about their employees and didn't expect them to wait for a miracle. She would be having the hard conversation later today with them—telling them all the details as transparently as possible so they could make the best decisions for themselves. She knew many of them, if not most, would need to start looking for other jobs.

"Alright, Jacqui, this is enough to bring to the team for now. We can work out the rest of the details later," said Kendra.

"Agreed."

"I'm going to go take five and then gather the team to give them the news."

"Kendra. You made the right decision."

Kendra gave her a pained smile and tapped the door frame on her way out. As she walked into her office, the phone rang, and she noticed it was Gil. But Gil, she knew no doubt, was told not to contact her. Curious, she picked up the phone.

"Hey, Gil," she said.

"Hey. Listen, I know I'm not supposed to call you. Actually, I wouldn't doubt that someone is listening in on this call and I'll be fired here shortly. But this is too important. The entire reason I started working for the USDA has been flushed down the toilet as of late, so I have nothing to lose.

"Anyway, first, I'm sorry how this has ended," Gil began.

"It's not over, Gil. It's never over and you know as well as I, that you can't talk that way, or it will be over," Kendra said.

"Fair, and that's probably the reason I called. I know you won't ever give up and there's a large part of me that isn't ready to give up either," said Gil.

"Good."

"I can't have the teams continue to feed their data into this mangled piece of what was once beautiful software to only turn out the garbage Our Great Leader is dictating. Do you see any way around this?"

"Absolutely. Don't do a thing."

"What?"

"Don't do anything."

"I'll say again—what? You just told me not to give up."

"And I'm not saying it now. You don't need to do anything, because the scientists that work for your Agency and others like it, will stop using it. Others may continue feeding it data but won't use the results. Because they know it's no longer science—it's propaganda, it's lies, it's manipulation. None of them got into science for that. They got into science to find out the truth. How this complex world actually works.

"They know Ecolution is compromised. Jack and Richard messed with the wrong people. You know as well as I do that those scientists won't engage the way Jack or the Administration thought or need them to. They will either continue finding the truth through their original methods or walk away altogether. You've read the news—some of them are already walking away. Some finding more success and being more effective than they've ever been," said Kendra.

"I should have figured it would be *you* making *me* feel better. I had also called to see how you were doing. How are you holding up?" asked Gil.

"I'd be lying if I said things were fine. Jacqui and I just got done devising a transition plan. We can stay open for another six months or so. But the attrition that will happen after I have a talk with the engineering group this afternoon will kill us before then."

"Sorry, Kendra. I wish there was more that I could do."

"I have always been successful persevering through things. I guess I finally met something I couldn't beat. But don't feel like you need to help me. Help yourself and the bigger fight. Although I deeply appreciate your concern and what you've already done for us, there's a bigger fight to have.

"I've come to realize it may not be all about truth either. The great philosopher-comedian, Sarah Silverman, recently said, 'You've never changed someone's mind by arguing, or facts. Facts don't change people's minds, as crazy as that sounds.' I couldn't agree more—it sounds insane. But, if facts don't change people's minds, what do you do? Move out of the Country? I can't stomach that—it feels like running away from the problem instead of trying to make it better. Ignore them? Too easy, and for how long? Until they upend our lives by taking away all our liberties? Live your own life? Cultivate your garden—as Voltaire suggests?

"The last response is the only one I can remotely stomach. Even with that one, though, I can't take literally—there's got to be more—more without rolling over and taking it. You read a lot of the same news I do. People are resisting and trying new things—they're cultivating their gardens. Looking back on why Jacqui and I started Evolve, we were cultivating our gardens. We all found ways we could cultivate ourselves and become more effective. As I'm talking I'm wondering why we're not evolving too.

"My garden was trampled and now it's time to either rebuild it or find some other fertile ground in which to cultivate a new garden. Don't worry about us, Gil, we'll figure it out. Perseverance has always served me well."

"No doubt you will, Kendra. Good luck to you two. I hope to be speaking with you again shortly. In the meantime, I'm going to cultivate my garden, too."

"Sounds good, Gil. Take care."

Kendra put the receiver down and sighed deeply. Her own talk gave her the perspective she needed. The rest of the day no longer felt like a chore to get through. It was simply a chance to pull some weeds and reseed—maybe with some new seeds this time around. She put her fidget cube down on her desk and headed out to the engineering area. There was no sense in delaying this discussion.

"Mike, please gather everyone over by the whiteboard in five minutes. I have a couple of announcements," Kendra said as she passed Mike's cube. Then she headed to the kitchen to refresh her coffee. When she returned, they were all standing next to the whiteboard where they met for their daily meetings and for impromptu design sessions on the whiteboard. It was conveniently located near enough to the engineers low-walled cubes, so they could hear discussions, but far enough that they could ignore them in case they needed to focus on their work.

Kendra let out a deep sigh and looked around the room at each one of her reports.

"Our contract with the USDA was terminated as of a couple of hours ago. I take full responsibility for why we lost it." Mike looked up at her with a sideways, questioning look.

"I imagine you all know what that means for the company as we don't currently have work in the pipeline that you can start on. I want to be as upfront and transparent as possible, so that you can make the right decisions for yourselves," continued Kendra.

"We have enough money in reserves to keep all of you on for the next six months. While I hope you do stay, Jacqui and I know it's too much to expect of you. You must take care of yourselves first, and if that means looking for other work, we understand.

"In fact, you are all more than welcome to use your time here to look for jobs, hone your skills, or do whatever you need. We will gladly continue to pay your salaries until you find new work. Most of you will simply roll out of bed in the morning and land a new job. You are all extremely talented.

"That said, Jacqui and I are not giving up. We are talking with groups we have in the pipeline to see if we can get earlier commitments from them. We're also talking with new groups, as well. Ecolution was a successful platform and regardless of what happened in our contract, it has caught the attention of a lot of other groups.

"We recognize this was a surprise. If I had known any earlier, I would have said something. But these things can happen quickly. This is now a good time to take a break, as well. Take a few days off or a week. Think about what you want to do."

Kendra was looking at each one as she spoke. The disappointment in their eyes was palpable. She knew how much she had let them down and was almost regretting her decision.

"I'm going to take a few days myself to think through options and see if we can't pull off a diving catch." As she looked around her team, most of them were looking down at the ground or off somewhere else. They looked like lost sheep without a shepherd.

"Does anyone have any questions?", she said.

Silence.

Retreat and Rethink

Kendra landed at the Seattle airport, SeaTac as the locals call it, just after three in the afternoon on Friday. She didn't like waiting at the baggage carousels, so she already had her light roller bag with her. She could head straight for the town car she booked. Friday traffic was starting to stack up, so it took nearly an hour to get dropped off at the ferry terminal near downtown Seattle. She didn't mind though—she came here to think.

Unused to the motion of the deck, she felt a bit wobbly stepping onto the deck from the passenger loading platform for the ferry. She soon got her bearings and headed up to the smaller, quieter passenger seating area on the top deck, picking the easternmost area so she could watch the Seattle skyline as the boat made its thirty-minute ride to Bainbridge Island. Kendra often liked people-watching on the ferries, but she chose the less populated, quiet area to continue her thinking.

Life seems to slow when you get on a ferry—at least most of the Puget Sound ferries. It was just what she needed.

Lisa and Blake were waiting for her when the ferry docked. By this time, she was completely relaxed.

"Hey munchkin," Lisa belted out through the crowd.

"It's so good to see you two!" Kendra answered back. "How are you?"

"Perfect, now that you're here. Hungry?" Blake asked.

"Famished," replied Kendra.

"Good, we have reservations at the Jack's Bistro in ten minutes, so let's get going"

"You two know just what I need. I love you!"

They made their way through the ferry traffic bottlenecked on Highway 305—the main thoroughfare to most of the rest of the island and the only way off it to the Kitsap Peninsula—and over to the gourmet restaurant set in a quaint, old house. It was some of the best food Kendra had ever known. Nothing in Colorado compared to it.

She and Nikolaj spent a Christmas and New Year's out on Bainbridge before her parents moved to Tucson a few years ago. While they were there, they attended a New Year's dinner at Jack's Bistro that included six courses and took over four hours to complete. It was heavenly and something she was sure she'd never forget. She couldn't wait to get a taste again.

They immediately ordered a bottle of wine and Kendra ordered the spring risotto and topped it off with the breaded pudding. It was just as she remembered it—absolutely divine.

"Lisa was telling me about your recent project. What was it called?" started Blake.

"Ecolution."

"Sorry, I meant to say, what *is* it called?", said Blake.

"No, you're right to say, what *was* it called. But I'll get to that in a minute. It's a software-as-a-service solution that helps government scientists pool and store their data, and scale up analysis," explained Kendra.

"Kendra, you gotta remember you're talking to a furniture designer and a children's book author. Say that again?" Lisa reminded her, referring to her husband and herself, respectively. They were both accomplished in their own right. It was just that their fields of expertise were vastly different than Kendra's unique background. Lisa had twelve young adult novels to her name, with her most recent trilogy making the New York Times Bestseller List. Blake was also doing well for himself, having designed several high-end furniture pieces that were selling well for the company he worked for.

"Sorry, apparently used to talking with these scientists who get offended if you don't make everything sound so complicated."

"No worries here. Dumb it down all you like. If you can come up with some analogy related to designing furniture, I might understand," Blake smiled.

"Ok, let's see. It's kinda like our favorite Swedish furniture store's build your own desk system, except you can come with your own parts"

"Uh, how could that ever work? Maybe that's too much of a stretch. I was just joking," Blake was doubtful.

"No, this works, stay with me. If your company made different parts of a desk, but each part was made so that it joined with the other parts in exactly the same way—like every desk leg has a two-inch round knob at the top which fits into a two-inch round hole in the base of the desktop. I'm sure that's not how you build furniture, but the point is, those interfaces all must meet the same specification. In the end, as long as they follow those specifications, you could have an almost infinite amount of combinations of legs, desktops, cabinets, hutches, whatever, right?"

"Yep, even I'm following," Lisa jumped in.

"So, instead of legs, desktops, cabinets, and hutches these scientists have input data, data filtering and validation, analyses and models, and output."

"And, again, backup, you lost me at input data. Maybe it's the wine," Blake sighed.

"Sorry, imagine I have a temperature gauge in a stream that takes measurements every hour. After one day, I have twenty-four temperature measurements. That is my input data. Now, I want to validate and maybe filter that data to make sure it's not giving me abnormal readings, like if the gauge was moved out of the water somehow and was taking air temperatures that were clearly higher than the water temperatures. The data filter would look at each value and say either, looks good or no that's wrong, we'll toss it out and not use it. Then I want to run some sort of program against the validated data to get some result. For example, given all my historic data for that stream gauge, is the temperature of the stream changing significantly over time?

"That's basically what Ecolution is, it's a glorified build-your-own-analysis-engine. The biggest advantage of it is that it allows a scientist to run thousands of these models simultaneously without having to pay much more. It used to be that a team of scientists could buy a few moderate sized computers to run their analyses on. But it usually wasn't enough to be able to run their models faster than a few days, weeks or even months. Ecolution, because it can create as many virtual instances of computers as it needs, it can run these analyses in a fraction of the time."

"Wow, that's incredible. I can't say that I completely understood what you were saying toward the end, but I understand the potential consequences. That's awesome," Lisa was clearly impressed. "But what's the problem then? You sounded pretty upset on the phone the other day."

"A few weeks ago, we noticed that all the analyses that have previously been saying, 'hey, we're in deep shit, look at this evidence of climate change!'—no one is seeing that anymore since they've started running their data through Ecolution. Something just didn't seem right—why would results all of a sudden change?

"So, Nikolaj's team pulled their data back out of the system and ran the analysis and got the same exact results as the model running in Ecolution. At that point, we at least knew that the models running in Ecolution were running as expected.

"Then a member of my team and another from Nikolaj's had the idea to send in some known data into the system and try to take it back out. They wondered if their data filters were changing the data in the wrong way. When they sent the values into the system and pulled them out everything was fine at first. But they realized the first batch of data they tested was data they had previously pulled from the system. So, they found some old data they knew produced results consistent with climate change—all the data points that would have caused the model to indicate climate change were altered to *not* result in climate change results!

"But they *knew* that their filter wasn't making those changes. All of their local tests with only their filter did not change the data in any way."

"Was someone else's filter altering their data?" Lisa asked.

"That was the weird thing. No other filters were registered to be applied to their data. We have automated tests that make sure this type of configuration is applied correctly.

"It was kind of a hair brained idea, but I suggested that the authentication filter which is applied to all data coming into the system to make sure it's coming from a trusted source, might be the culprit. So, we asked for the source code from the security team at the USDA to see if we could rule that out. They won't give it to us. They told us that for government security reasons, the source code cannot be shared with contractors. We went to his boss who I know well. He was willing to help but was immediately overruled by the Deputy Directory several levels above him. No one seems to know how the guy got involved or why at his level."

"Jeebus," Blake said, barely audible.

"Amen. This sounds like top-level spy shit," Lisa added.

"Funny you say that. We ended up writing some code in our product that watched out for changes in the data. Anything that changed the data was captured along with details of the code that changed it. We found that the security module contained an elaborate algorithm for filtering and normalizing the data. It shouldn't have been doing *anything* to the data. That filter was *only* intended to make sure the data was coming from a trusted source.

"As soon as we found conclusive evidence, they also figured out what we were doing. We made the mistake of trying to pass that information out of their network to ours and they caught it. Luckily, we created another back door to get the data. But in the meantime, they realized what we were doing and cancelled our contract.

"That was currently our only revenue for Evolve. We have a little left in reserves, but that will only take us into the next half of the year. So, this is where

I'm struggling. I've always could persevere through these types of things—no matter how hard. But we're out of options this time."

"No shit," said Lisa. "I'm sorry."

"Meanwhile the FBI got involved and was investigating two of the people involved in this whole thing. They found enough evidence to charge them. So, now Congress is also investigating since it involves government employees charged with a crime. They just called while I was at the airport and invited me to testify before the Senate's Commerce, Science, and Transportation Committee."

"That's a weird combination of responsibilities for a committee," said Blake.

"I know, right? And at least they didn't subpoena me—I do have the option to say no. But that's not something I want to deal with at the moment, given the fact that I'm losing something I've spent so much time building."

"You can't accept," Lisa said flatly. "You have seen what's going on with this new administration. They're replacing people left and right with those who are suppressing the truth and denying things the rest of us have accepted as fact, like climate change. They've been forcing other people out, censoring out 'climate change' from government scientists. And now they're going so far as to alter data, so it doesn't show climate change. They will eat you alive, Kendra. They'll crush you and not look back. You cannot say anything!" Lisa was almost in hysterics by the time she finished. Her fear of what was going on in the government was growing daily as she read the news. Now she was afraid that what she read about was going to happen to one of her best friends, too.

2

Lisa and Blake had a tiny eighty square foot hut that Lisa used to write in. It was a converted storage shed with a whole top-half of one wall replaced with glass that wrapped around part of the other two sides. Sitting at the built-in desk Lisa had a full 180-degree view of the forest around her and the Puget Sound in front of her. A mini wood burning stove kept the hut warm during winter days, and a fold-down bed was perfect for naps. It was also the perfect spot for Kendra to do some thinking.

She woke up early on Saturday morning, crept out to the kitchen, and made herself a pot of coffee. Then, she grabbed her notebook, a thermos full of coffee, and headed out to the converted shed.

It was incredibly peaceful—exactly what she needed. At first, she just sat and took it all in. The forest was dense, but she had a tiny glimpse of the Sound to look out on. The water was as calm as it ever gets, and no one was out on it yet. Out in the distance, she could see a golden eagle circling.

After a time, her mind came back to the issue— should she accept the invitation to testify before the Senate? Although she wasn't as terrified as Lisa, she didn't see any benefit for her to accept. *What would I get out of several hours—actually, days—of stress?* she thought. *It's not like I'm going to win back that contract. Or would I? When have you ever given up before the final buzzer? Though in this case the buzzer has already rung.*

She let her mind wander between Nikolaj, Evolve, the hearing, and various systems of logic. She often thought about logic and thought systems when trying to think through an important issue. This time she kept coming back to lateral and scaled thinking. *Is it because I've hit a dead end for once*, she thought. *Is there really no way to push through this straight ahead? If that's the case, what can I do to succeed in some other way maybe in an even bigger way?*

Then it hit her, why hadn't she thought about this before. Her whole world had changed around her over the past year, dramatically so in the past week. *I can no longer play the same game and win. I must play a different game or even make up my own game. And there are millions of people like me struggling with the same thing—that's my scale.*

Kendra knew this was what she needed—and it took her less than an hour to figure it out. She scribbled a few notes in her notebook. The small wood stove was heating up the hut nicely at this point. She turned around, curled up on the bed attached to the wall, and fell back to sleep. She was going to accept the hearing invite.

The Hearing

Kendra had prepared herself for the experience, watching video of hearing testimonies and reading through transcripts. But as soon as the doors opened revealing the Senate Hearing Chambers, the sheer visual stimulation took her breath away.

There were several rows of seats in the back of the room where she entered, enough to seat around a hundred. In front of that was a long wooden desk where a nameplate for her sat, along with the three other witnesses. The desk looked tiny in the vast hearing chamber, but she knew it was plenty big. Set back about twenty feet in front of the desk was a three-sided, wooden paneled section where the Senators would sit, purposely several feet higher than she. If anything was designed to intimidate, it was this room. The most prominent and unexpected items were the thirty or so reporters seated and kneeling on the floor in front of the Senators' panel— all with cameras. If there weren't enough people already, there were another two rows of seats behind the Senators—presumably for their aides— approximately forty of them. A large video camera protruded from an opening in the massive marble wall in the back of the room, resembling the projector in a movie theater, but recording everything that went on in the room instead of playing it back. Kendra thought about how it would stare at her, capturing every minute expression and word she uttered, recording it for eternity. Kendra was the movie.

Take a deep breath, Kendra. Head high. You own this, Kendra thought to herself. *5-4-3-2-1.* She straightened up and seemed to grow an inch or two. Her face relaxed and she began walking forward, looking straight ahead toward the middle seats where the Committee Chair would sit. Feeling what seemed like a hundred pair of eyeballs on her, she made it to the long desk with four seats. The other three seats were already filled. The empty seat with her nameplate in front was on the far left. To her right sat Alice Hooper who stood up with a broad smile and extended hand as soon as she saw Kendra arrive at her seat.

"Hi, you must be Dr. Williams, I'm Dr. Alice Hooper. It's nice to meet you," said Alice.

"Very nice to meet you, as well. But no doctor as part of my name," said Kendra.

Tom Lloyd and Janet Turnball also stood up after hearing the greetings.

"Dr. Tom Lloyd," extending a hand.

"And Dr. Janet Turnball," said Janet.

"Do you all know each other," said Kendra.

"Not until last night," said Tom. "We met downstairs in the hotel lobby at the Hampton. None of us are high-rollers. Sorry we missed you."

"That's alright. I didn't get in until late last night anyway and staying just down the road at the Hilton Garden Inn—also not a high roller." They all laughed.

The room got quiet and everyone else stood. Kendra took another deep breath. *Here we go, remember you control the tempo,* she reminded herself. She saw Senator Thomas Wilson walking toward his throne in the middle, followed by Senators Beake and Talbot. The Senators sat down and as if choreographed the entire chamber settled into their positions.

"The meeting of the Senate Committee on Commerce, Science, and Transportation will come to order," said Senator Wilson. After a few seconds of shuffling as people took their seats, he continued. "We're here this morning to discuss the potential censorship of scientific data, its impact to our scientific community, and ultimately how it impacts the legislation and policies we make.

"Ms. Williams, Drs. Hooper, Turnball, and Lloyd, we welcome you and we welcome all the folks attending this meeting. It's almost overwhelming to see the number of people interested in this topic."

Almost overwhelming? thought Kendra.

"We asked each one of you here today as part of our investigation into several charges of scientific censorship, including one involving criminal intent. As you know, it is our duty as Senators to look into charges against public officials to determine if laws or policies must change or be created.

"I will, however, remind you, Ms. Williams, that you are not without guilt and knowingly broke the contract you entered into with the U.S. Government. I assume you will not forget that." Senator Wilson looked down at her over his reading glasses hanging off the bottom of his nose, as if to emphasize this point and his disapproval. Kendra looked him directly in the eyes without expression.

"Ms. Williams, let's begin with you. Would you please state for the record who you are, the company you work for, and the software your company built for the U.S. Government," Senator Wilson said.

"My name is Kendra Williams. I am the Chief Technology Officer of a software company named Evolve Inc. Until a couple of weeks ago we were under contract with the U.S. Department of Agriculture and U.S. Geological Survey to create a scientific computing platform to improve the efficiency of scientific data collection and analysis for the agencies. Our platform allowed scientists to run their models in scalable, cloud computing environments that decreased time to results by a factor of over a thousand. Scientists now wait minutes to hours for results that previously took them weeks and months to otherwise compute. The impact of these improvements meant that scientists can churn out scientific reports and publish papers at a much faster rate. This would have allowed policy makers—Senators such as yourselves—a much quicker stream of information in which to make more timely decisions."

"Really, Ms. Williams, an improvement by a factor of over a thousand? That seems like an extreme claim", said Senator Wilson.

"It is not. I don't make hyperbolic claims. I am happy to show you the data."

"Fine, fine, that won't be necessary at this time, but we may want to revisit that data in another forum. Based on the memo provided by the FBI regarding their investigation into Dr. Denning and Mr. Knight, we understand you became suspicious of some of the data processed by your own software. Would you describe the events leading up to the point at which you became suspicious and the steps you took to investigate the issues?"

Kendra spent the next twenty minutes describing in detail the story she had told so many others. She had rehearsed her story with Nikolaj and knew all the facts. She left out no details including all the facts she knew were in breach of their contract. Her goal was to be completely honest. Just as she likes to run a company and her life, she knew these Senators needed the whole truth to make accurate decisions about policies and potential new laws.

"Ms. Williams," said Senator Beake, "we spend much of our time in these seats asking questions and attempting to read through the lines of people who dance around issues and are worried they might say the wrong thing. You, on the other hand, have given us all the raw facts you thought were relevant, regardless of their potential negative impact on you. Why be so honest with us given the potential consequences? Your future customers could be watching this hearing."

Oh, the three people watching C-SPAN right now? Two of whom are beginning to nod off and the third playing solitaire, she thought. "I have long been a proponent of letting scientific evidence stand on its own. I believe that scientific evidence is in and of itself the truth on which reasonable people will make decisions. Science and fact are critical to the health and longevity of our society. Difference of opinion are tolerable and required. But active undermining and attack are not acceptable. Science, reason, truth, and fact will prevail in the end whether we embrace it or not. If we chose to ignore it, it will be at our own peril. If we chose to embrace it, we will at least have a chance to figure out how to react to it. As Winston Churchill said, 'The truth is incontrovertible. Malice may attack it, ignorance may deride it, but in the end, there it is. '"

"Thank you, Ms. Williams, for your testimony. One last question before we turn to Dr. Hooper. Your involvement in this investigative hearing was purely voluntary and, as far as I can tell, provides you no reward. In fact, based on your testimony, it may be a detriment to future work for your company. What made you testify here today?", Senator Talbot asked.

This was the opening she was waiting for.

"I've continued to live my life as if nothing changed or possibly that there wasn't much I could do about it. Yet all around us the paradigms we've grown used to have been whittled away. Sure, things always change, but not at this scale and not so drastically. What happens to species when they don't change and the environment around them does? They eventually go extinct. As we go through life we must be different people as we grow and mature, as the people and situations we live in change. We often feel stuck in jobs that we don't enjoy, not realizing that with a little effort we can go find a new one that would be a much better fit. Or that we could do something completely different.

"This is one of those moments where bigger change is needed; where I now realize I need to do things differently and possibly become a different person. I have always lived under the rule that I must persevere through adversity. While there is still a grain of truth to that, I also realize that it's not enough. It's time for me to do something different to be successful and have an impact. It's time for me to realize that I can have an impact on my changing world. I don't yet know what that is that I will do, but I intend to figure that out soon."

Out of the corner of her eye, she saw Alice, Janet, and Tom all looking at her with understanding and gratitude. As if this was the answer they had been struggling to find, as well. Kendra laid it out in front of them in one simple answer. The truth, Kendra knew, was that she struggled to find the answer too and everything within her fought against it.

The hearing continued with testimony from Alice, Janet, and Tom. All three appeared relaxed, as if they had been granted a second chance.

ERIK STEVENSON

Turning Tide

Kendra's testimony was reprinted in several of the national newspapers. The articles empowered more and more people across the country to stand up and put an assertive voice to their convictions. They realized there was no need to sit back and wait for things to improve. This was their country too.

Kendra received thousands of emails of congratulations, support, and thanks. A lot of people had started to give up hope. But Kendra's testimony changed all that for them. Knowing that others out there were struggling with the same issues gave them hope. And, Kendra provided a means for them to act. It was comforting to many to realize they had so many more options than to hope someone else fixed the problem for them. There were now things they could do to.

The news quickly started to reflect this as people began to act.

2

Dr. Tom Lloyd sat across from his former boss Bob Reynolds. This time they were recording a new episode of Bob's new podcast Government of Science. They were having much the same conversation as they were having before they were both unceremoniously fired by the USGS. But this time they were enjoying it.

"Welcome back to a new episode of the Government of Science. Today my guest is Dr. Tom Lloyd, previously a top scientist at the Northwest Climate Science Center and an ex-colleague of mine. Tom it's a great pleasure to have you on the show," began Bob.

"Thanks for having me, Bob," answered Tom.

"Now, you and I haven't always seen eye to eye on the government's role in science, so I thought what better topic for us to discuss," Bob continued tongue-in-cheek.

"Ain't that the truth," Tom returned.

"But before we get into that, Tom, tell us a bit about what you're up to these days now that you're no longer working at the Northwest Climate Science Center. I heard something about Alexander Hamilton."

"If I could come remotely close to a fraction of the influence Hamilton had on our Country, I would be happy. Back in his day Hamilton wrote a lot, and I mean a lot, of opinion pieces that he wrote into newspapers. Mostly around how he thought the government should be formed and what role it should take. My intent is to do much the same thing but offering my opinion instead on what role our government should have in the pursuit of science. Should it have a role at all? If so, what should it be?

Unlike Hamilton, however, I don't write under various pseudonyms."

"And where can we find some of your writings?"

"Various places. I've written pieces for the Guardian, ScienceDaily, and a Conversation on Edge.org."

"Great and I imagine this will be a good segue but introduce us to one of your favorite opinion topics."

"I'd love to. I mostly focused on the separation between science, specifically scientific reporting by government researchers, and their governing bodies. My premise is that government bodies should have no say in how or what researchers report of their findings. For example, if I run an experiment that shows climate change, the agency I work for or the administration it's running under should have no power to dictate whether I publish my results, what my results were, or the words I use to describe my results.

"So, if the current administration does not believe that climate change is occurring, and that people of this country should not be guided by science effectively performed by the government, they still should have no say as to what verbiage is used in their own publications?

"Absolutely not. Does President Holloway get to dictate anything that Justice Andrews writes in her opinions? Now, granted, science within our form of government is performed exclusively by agencies under the order of the President and not in a separate branch of government. But should it? Should the Executive Branch dictate what truth and facts are? Isn't that what science acknowledges? That we don't always know the truth, but we can discover it through scientific methods. Truth has no political bend, nor is it owned by any one party. Science and truth are apolitical, they stand alone."

Bob and Tom continued their debate and Bob's podcast subscribers swelled beyond his expectations. Who knew that so many people were interested in how the government did science and how it was controlled—or not.

3

Mark Sanderson was still working in the Bayview Oxbow and Starr Creek Preserves toward the end of the summer. He was wrapping up his field work for his thesis. Dr. Alice Hooper was no longer at the field station, though he spoke with her occasionally. She ably continued to serve as his advisor and help him with his research.

Jane Hemsworth the former CEO of Bitserv, a blockchain implementation service provider, contacted the office in which Dr. Hooper used to work. She heard that Dr. Hooper was the foremost expert in coastal changes related to climate change and wanted to hear more about her research. After years in the tech industry, Jane was ready to make some more meaningful impacts with the vast fortune she made. She was informed that Dr. Hooper was no longer with the agency, but that Mark was available. She reluctantly accepted.

Jane arrived at Mark's office early on the morning of August 24th. The same man from the DC office was there to accompany them.

"Hi Jane, I am Mark Sanderson, and this is Joe Pistelli," Marked began.

"It's nice to meet you Mark. Can I ask you why Dr. Hooper no longer works here?" Jane asked, accustomed to getting straight to the point and finding the truth.

Joe immediately cut off Mark. "Dr. Hooper moved onto other work. We're here to show you the reserves and provide a bit of their history."

"I'm not interested in their history, Joe. I am here to learn about the effects of climate change on coastal ecology," Jane was already annoyed.

"The EPA is not in the business of climate change research as it is conjecture and not related to coastal ecology," Joe began. Mark rolled his eyes and Jane noticed.

"Joe, it's clear that you're full of shit and simply here to make sure Mark doesn't say anything the EPA—or shall I say, it's unorthodox, unqualified Administrator—doesn't want to admit to because it doesn't fit with his own give-me-what-I-deserve agenda. I realize you and your cronies don't want to talk about the truth. You're only there to facilitate the removal of protections borne out of solid science.

"Mark, follow me, we have some real talking to do."

Mark was more than happy to follow Jane's lead. He had had enough of Joe.

"Mark, you walk out this door and you have no future with the EPA," Joe threatened.

"There was no future for me here anyway," Mark answered.

Mark jumped in behind Jane in the back of her rented black GMC Yukon. Although fewer people accompanied her than did when she was CEO, Jane still enjoyed the company of a driver and assistant in her travels. The driver closed the door behind Mark and jumped in himself, with Joe still yelling as they drove off.

"Apologies, Mark. I'm not used to wasting my time and it appeared that's where that conversation was headed. I also realize the irony of me traveling in this enormous vehicle to come talk to you about climate change and ecology," Jane said.

"No worries. In fact, thank you. I needed an excuse to get out of there. I had been afraid of ruining my career before. But was beginning to realize there was no future for me there anyway— not one that I could make a positive impact with anyway. I now fully understand why Alice left. Speaking of whom, I suggest we go see her. Her new Institute is right up the road. She'll be able to give you much better information than I," Mark answered, sounding quite relieved.

"I appreciate that, Mark. Let's go see Alice."

4

Dr. Alice Hooper founded the Coastal Change Institute after listening to Kendra's testimony and realizing she was no longer effective in her position and subsequently left the Environmental Protection Agency. She now provided global consultancy and taught online courses on the effects of climate change on coastline ecologies. One of her first students was Alexander Morrison. Alexander provided the funding Alice needed to get the Institute started. They spoke often, not because Alexander wanted to direct Dr. Hooper's efforts, but because he wanted to learn about the science himself.

When Mark, Jane and her small entourage entered the building housing Alice's Institute, she was on a video conference with Alexander. Alice's office was encased in glass and Alexander also saw from Alice's video camera who walked in. Alexander and Jane met on several occasions in the past when they both worked in the tech industry.

"Well, look who the cat dragged in," drawled Alexander.

"Hey, if it isn't my favorite billionaire," Jane responded jovially.

"I guess you two know each other," Alice interjected.

'Sorry, Dr. Hooper," Mark said, "This is Jane Hemsworth, former CEO of Bitserv."

"Oh, of course, I have read about you several times, Jane. I think the last was about how blockchain technology was being adopted in a myriad other industries beyond financial transactions. It's a pleasure to meet you," Alice said respectfully.

"And a pleasure to meet you, as well. I've read several of your recent papers on coastal ecology and climate change. I intended to meet you today but was lucky enough to start with Mark. His eye roll told me all I needed to know about our friend Joe. Had you met Joe before you left the EPA?" Jane said, winking at Mark.

Mark blushed and was feeling a bit star struck. Two apparently famous tech leaders along with his revered advisor, Dr. Hooper. This day turned out much better than expected.

Alexander spoke up from the screen behind Alice, "well, it looks like you three have plenty to talk about. Alice, let's catch up again on Monday of next week. I'd like to continue our discussion about submerged aquatic vegetation and how it relates to climate change and effects on commercial fish and crab species. Jane, good to see you. Both of you let me know if there is anything I can help with. Later." And Alexander was out.

Jane laughed. "He can go from talking tech to spewing words like 'submerged aquatic vegetation' without skipping a beat."

"I'm very grateful to Alexander, he's made all this possible," Alice replied opening her arms as if to show off the place. "I feel like I'm making a positive impact on my discipline again."

"Well, let's get down to business. Maybe I can help you make an even larger impact. And, I believe, Mark may now have a little bit more time on his hands to help here, too."

Alice smiled, "Mark, I'm proud of you. I know how hard it must have been for you to walk out of there and not look back. I can't imagine having done that at that stage in my career. But I hope to make it all worth it for you. I've learned over the past couple of months that there are other ways to still do science—the right way."

Although it was not how either of them ever envisioned their careers as scientists, Alice and Mark had both found ways to positively impact coastal ecology science.

5

Dr. Janet Turnball had made it to Barcelona after all. After arriving at the airport in Boston and learning that the bastards on high had cancelled her original airline ticket and hotel reservations to keep her from going to the United Nations Climate Change Conference, she booked her own ticket. When she arrived in Barcelona she contacted an old colleague who had moved back home to Barcelona and stayed with her during the week.

After meeting Kendra, Janet realized it was time for her to change tactics, as well. On the flight from Boston, she had nearly decided to retire. She was done dealing with the bullshit between the university

185

and the government. But by the following day she decided she wasn't ready to retire, but she was done with her current job.

In Barcelona she had met Dr. Grete Karlsen from the University of Oslo. Grete studied the social dimensions of climate change. She had explained to Janet that Oslo was becoming a popular place for new startups. Janet realized that was exactly what she wanted to do. She called Dr. Karlsen and pumped her for more information on who to contact and how to immigrate to Norway.

By the time the week was out she had a plan. She spent the next few days finalizing all the details she needed to move to Oslo and start her new business. She was going to open AgriDaption to help farmers in areas highly vulnerable to the effects of climate change, adopt practices to help them adapt to new and changing conditions. Grete joined her as a co-founder.

Final Wave

It had been a few months since Kendra had given her testimony to the Senate Subcommittee. Evolve had only a couple of months' worth of cash reserves remaining. But still Kendra's team continued to come in each day. People did spend the occasional moment perusing job listings, but little enthusiasm was shown, and most jobs didn't entice enough to be applied to. Much of their time was spent adding the cool new features they had wanted to add to Ecolution but previously didn't have the time to work on. There was also the occasional side project one or more of them would start, often just to see if they could pull it off. It was clear they didn't want to give up the good thing they had.

Kendra was listening to the banter out on the engineering floor and thinking about how much she was going to miss it.

"Mike, you headed up to see Cat again tonight?", teased Peter.

Mike slipped him a quick glance.

"That's getting to be pretty much every night now," said Peter.

"Yeah, but honestly that drive is killing me."

"Why don't you just move up there?"

"Jeez, what's with all the sad faces? What did the Grinch say? There will be no sad faces on Christmas," Jacqui interrupted with her best Grinch impersonation.

"Jacqui, as much as I love you, you definitely need to work on your Grinch impersonations and it's noooowhere near Christmas. God, I do love that movie though. Jury duty, jury duty, pink slip, blackmail, eviction letter, jury duty, jury duty", said Peter.

"You know, if you spent as much time writing code as you do practicing *your* Grinch impersonations, you'd be an amazing developer," said Jacqui.

"Heeeyyyoooooo," laughed Katie.

Peter nodded in agreement and shrugged as everyone else joined in the laughter.

"Anywho," Jacqui continued. "I just got off the phone with Alice Hooper from the from the Coastal Change Institute. If you remember she and Kendra testified together in that Senate Hearing a few months ago."

Kendra's ears perked. She had been in touch with Alice a few times since the hearing and had developed a strong bond. She didn't realize Jacqui was talking with her too.

"Later this week we will be signing a deal to continue our work with Ecolution."

All heads turned up to look at Jacqui and over to Kendra as if to double check that one parent wasn't trying to pull something over on the kids.

"Really?" asked Mike.

"Really," Jacqui answered. "She obviously heard about Ecolution during the hearing, loved the idea, and had spoken with Kendra a few times since about it. She recently parted with the EPA and founded the Coastal Change Institute, so she could continue her work in more effective ways. She suffered through censorship in other ways than we did at the EPA, got fed up with it, and left. Tech billionaire Alexander Morrison and Jane Hemsworth, former CEO of Bitserv, teamed up to invest in Alice's Institute."

Heads began nodding in recognition of those two names. They had all heard of them and envied them.

"Alice convinced Alexander and Jane to put some money toward Ecolution. Both of them also have investments in various other similar companies and institutes and are considering expanding Ecolution's use with those companies, as well. Alexander's connections with several cloud service providers make scaling this out simple. This could really be huge for us!" said Jacqui.

"Yeah, baby!" yelled Peter.

Kendra was speechless. She had spoken with Alice a few times before and they had joked about the possibility of rebuilding Ecolution, but Kendra thought it was just that—joking.

"I can see some of you are hesitant to be excited and I don't blame you. Kendra and I had spent a lot of time trying to figure out how to keep the company afloat as long as possible, assuming we'd eventually have to close the doors in the next couple of months.

Now I come in to tell you were just fine—probably better than fine."

"This is wonderful news. This calls for a celebration. How about lunch at Salt?" said Kendra.

"Ooh, fancy," said Katie.

The mention of food and drinks convinced the rest of them that this truly was a cause for celebration. After living with the thought that the company was going under, they were hesitant to believe just the opposite.

As Kendra and Jacqui walked toward the door together, Jacqui leaned into whisper to Kendra.

"Alice did all this legwork and called because of you and your testimony. She thought it was brilliant and couldn't agree more with the call to action. She'd been searching for that call herself but was thankful that you so eloquently spoke about it for so many others to hear. She hadn't wanted to get your hopes up over the last couple of months as she was working out the details. In fact, she wanted to tell you first. I just couldn't help myself," said Jacqui.

"I'm just thankful it came when it did. Any later and we would have started losing some of them. There all tremendously talented," said Kendra.

"They are."

2

The team spent a long lunch at Salt, which ended with Jacqui buying one final round. There was a spattering of different beer orders, a martini or two, and a few brave souls who ordered straight up whiskey. They had all quickly cheered up after warming up to the idea that their jobs were once again secure.

"I need to head back to the office to wrap up some things, but Jacqui and I wanted to say thank you for all the great work you have done," Kendra started. "We know working for a small company can have its ups and downs—we certainly experienced that recently. At the same time, we see great things on the horizon. Jacqui filled me in on some of the details of the deal with the Coastal Change Institute and what else may come out of it. We don't want to get everyone's hopes up artificially, but if half of it works out we will likely be expanding.

"Please take the rest of the day to do whatever you all want and let's all start fresh tomorrow. If I know some of you, that doesn't need to be too early in the morning," Kendra said, shooting a glance and smirk over to Peter.

"Wait, what? Why are you looking at me?" Peter said, and everyone laughed.

"Feel free to expense another round on us, but the rest will have to be on your own. You all have a good rest of the day and, again, thank you. You are an awesome team, and this would be impossible without all of you," said Kendra as she stood to leave.

Jacqui also said a heartfelt thank you and left with Kendra. They walked back through the lunch crowds in the mall and back up to the office.

"Jacqui, thank you too. Running this company with you has been one of the most rewarding things I've done in my life. I couldn't ask for a better partner," said Kendra just as they were heading into their own offices.

"I couldn't agree more. Today is the reason we got into this. We're going to be able to help a lot of people with our software and we're going to continue to keep a lot of great people employed," Jacqui replied.

They both went into their offices and sunk into their chairs. There were simultaneous sighs and then they were quickly back at it. There was a lot of work to be done to get contracts prepared, start setting up preliminary meetings, and finding productive work for the team to do during the transition period.

Kendra wrapped up a little early and decided to go pick up some groceries so she and Nikolaj could celebrate tonight. On her way out, she noticed Mike was back sitting at his desk, so she went over to see what he was up to.

"Everything OK, Mike?" Kendra asked.

Mike looked up smiling. "Absolutely. That was some great news today. I'm super excited. There were a few things I had wanted to do with Ecolution that would have been useful for the USDA work, but never got prioritized. Looking at what the Coastal Change Institute does, I think this will help them, too. Just thought I'd do a little work on some of it, since I know we'll have a bit of transition time."

"I should have known," Kendra responded smiling. "Why don't you work with the team tomorrow to put together a proposed short release of the features you all have been wanting to add. Let's make it for one month out—we should have a contract in place by then. You and I had talked about the continuous deployment initiative, as well. Let's see if we can fit some of the groundwork for that in there."

"Consider it done," said Mike. "Oh, and have you seen this," he said turning toward his computer and bringing up his news feed. He clicked on the top story with the headline, "Two Government Employees Guilty of Fraud in Software Hacking Case." Kendra saw pictures of Jack and Richard in the top-left of the page, just under the headline. She didn't have to read it to know the details—she knew Special Agent Jason Wellington got what he was looking for.

"Well, well. They got what they deserve," Kendra said.

"Yeah, that's good news. You think we'll get that contract back?" Mike asked.

"Possibly, but I'm not going to hold my breath. It will take them a while to unravel everything and…"

"Kendra, Gil's on line one. You'll want to take it from your office," they heard Jacqui shouting from down the hall.

"Alright, Mike, I need to take this. Go home early and have a good night. If you really want to work on this, go work from home," Kendra said as she headed back to office.

"Sure, you too. And, Kendra."

"Yes?"

"I wouldn't have left even if all the money ran out. You and Jacqui would have found us work eventually. And what we're doing here is just too important to walk away from."

All Kendra could do was smile back.

3

Kendra threw her bag back in one of the chairs in her office and picked up the receiver. For about the hundredth time today, she let out a deep sigh, then hit the button for line one.

"Hey, Gil. What's up?" said Kendra.

"I have some good news, too. Did you hear the news about Jack and Richard?"

"Yes."

"Well, the best part of that is that we can re-enact your contract."

"What? Great, but I assume though that it will be months before we can get back to work on it, right?"

"No, it's done. It's done as of ten minutes ago. I still had control over the contract. Jack overrode me earlier, but all his actions were nulled retroactively over the past six months. They'll also be examining other actions he was a part of, but they made an across the board decision so that his immediate staff weren't hamstrung in the meantime."

"Wow, that *is* great news. We're going to have to hire more engineers," she said the last sentence almost to herself.

"Sorry?"

"Oh, nothing. Thinking out loud. Thanks so much, Gil. I'll give you a call first thing tomorrow morning to reset and we can start from there."

"Sounds good."

"Thanks again, Gil. Bye."

She put the receiver down and sighed once again.

"Jacqui!" she yelled, forgetting Mike was also down the hall. "We got the USDA contract back! We start tomorrow!"

Mike heard and smiled.

"Holy shit!" Jacqui yelled back.

Mike chuckled, and his smile broadened.

4

Kendra walked back home over to and down 14th Street, passing the bandshell in Central Park. She walked slowly enjoying the slight nip in the fall air. It was starting to cool off now, though without a doubt they will likely have another warm spell or two before fall turns to winter. She would probably have to start keeping her bedroom window closed soon so as not to waste electricity on heating an open house. She'd probably still sneak in a cracked window every once in a while, to enjoy the cool crisp air.

She then made her way across to Oats and Barley Market where she picked up a couple of nice filet mignons, some carrots, and fingerling potatoes of various colors. She knew they already had some dried porcini mushrooms at home to grind up to season the steaks, and garlic and chives for the potatoes—mashed of course. Mashed orange, yellow, and blue fingerling potatoes were a perfect fall complement. The carrots could probably just be thrown in with the steaks in the frying pan to cook. They also had a good bottle of cabernet sauvignon at home that would go well with the meal.

After paying for her groceries and stuffing them into her backpack, she headed down the last couple of blocks back home. Coda greeted her at the door, tail whipping around in a circle. After a good petting, he ran back to the laundry room and returned with a sock, dropping it and looking at her from a safe distance. He looked at her like, *hey look what I have, I know I'm not supposed to have it, are you going to chase me now!?* Kendra just sighed, she was too content to be upset. She just looked back at him and said, "you know you're not supposed to have that, but you're also too damn cute to do anything about it at the moment—and I'm talking to a dog again. Alright, I bet you need to go outside. Out you go," she said as she opened the back door to let him out.

"Alexa, play Chopin on the radio," said Kendra as she started getting out all the ingredients and cookware she needed to start dinner.

"Getting your Chopin station," Alexa responded.

"Thank you. And now I'm talking to a black cylinder. Between you and Coda I've lost it."

Just then she heard Nikolaj's car pull into the side driveway and a few seconds later him bounding up the creaky front steps. He came in the door looking happy but somewhat hesitant. They had both had a hard week. He clearly had news but wanted to be sensitive to what she was dealing with. Then he noticed the spread.

"What's this for? Did you already hear about my news?" Nikolaj asked.

"No! What news?" she said.

"Out of the blue, an Alexander Morrison, who's some big tech billionaire and now investor, called to tell me he wants to replace all the previous funding I'd lost from my government sources! Can you believe it?"

A broad wide smile swept across her face as he said it. "I can believe it, and I'm so happy for you," she said.

"But you didn't already know? What are the filet mignons for?"

"Coincidentally, another organization, the Coastal Change Institute, who Alexander also invests in, called wanting to purchase Ecolution."

"Are you kidding me? That's wonderful. You went into work this morning thinking you were going to have to start letting some of your team go. Now you should be good for a little while longer."

"Apparently a lot while longer. They have piqued the interest of several other similar organizations who are also expressing interest in Ecolution. This could be huge!"

"I'm so happy for you, hon. This is well deserved."

"Same to you. Now let's get this food going, I'm starving. Open up that bottle of wine and pour me a glass, would you?"

Everything felt so good and so right. Losing the contract felt like a bombshell—tonight was the reward for everything they worked for. It was that feeling you get after a long struggle when the reward is finally paid out. Kendra knew there was never absolute certainty in the world. Just because she worked hard didn't guarantee her success. But she knew she lived in the world of probability, and if you stack the odds in your favor you have a much better chance of winning. Although an evil genius, she always appreciated what Auric Goldfinger in the James Bond film of his name, said about stacking odds in one's favor. She never wanted to be immoral about it or take advantage of anyone—her goal was simply to do good, productive work that would increase the chance of her success. Like giving it her best at the end of a field hockey game even if they were down or trying to find the company work even when it looked dismal.

They sat down to dinner with Chopin still playing in the background, Coda laying under the table at their feet, and beautiful plates of porcini encrusted filet mignon, garlic-chive mashed potatoes, and roasted carrots. Two fresh glasses of cabernet sat next to their plates, and three candles were lit in the middle of their small table for two. They both sighed and simultaneously raised their glasses and said, "Congratulations."

Once the contentment of good food set in, Nikolaj spoke.

"The Dean paid me a visit today."

"Oh?"

"He mentioned that he read your reprinted testimony in the Times. Said he thought it was timely and thought you eloquently said what most of us professors had difficulty saying."

"Nice of him."

"Yeah, wondered if you had any interest in teaching a couple of classes on Science, Ethics, and Policy,"

"Yes."

"But I told him you wouldn't be interested."

"No, I am."

"That you needed…"

"Nikolaj! Yes! Yes, I'm interested." Nikolaj looked up, startled.

"Wait, what?" he said.

"I have spent the greater part of my life banging my head against the wall. Always working harder, persevering through things until I finally won—or lost altogether. I just got done telling people they needed to look at things differently and consider alternative approaches. That life isn't always the same and we need to adjust. I need to walk my talk.

And what better way than to share those ideas with others? I want to do this, Nikolaj.

"It also solves a lot of problems. You're exhausted from that commute. There's no need for that anymore. Let's move back to Fort Collins. I can probably even continue at least some of my involvement in Evolve. There's no reason I couldn't work remotely. And frankly, I bet Mike wouldn't mind spending more time up in Fort Collins. We could start a satellite office and he could spend more time with Cat.

"We could also sell this house or rent it out and make a little money. Getting out of Boulder would save us a ton of money. I'll come up with you tomorrow and talk to the Dean."

"Ok. Wow. I'm in. Let's do this."

Kendra smiled and returned to her dinner. They spent the rest of the dinner in silence—not the silence of *I don't know what to say*, but the silence of contentment and understanding. That silence you can only find with someone you know well and are at complete ease with. The food was amazing; the company was amazing; and their lives were just how they wanted them to be.

After finishing dinner, they cleaned up and wandered into the living room where Coda was contentedly curled up on the couch with his eyes closed. Nikolaj looked at his two guitars, one acoustic and the other electric, trying to decide what he wanted to play. He chose his Stedman Pro Stratocaster electric but didn't plug it in. He had recently bought it to try something different and was pleasantly surprised how much fun he had with it. At the end of a day, it was like a musical kind of meditation. He rifled through some of his finger warm ups and a couple of his favorite licks like the beginning of John Mayer's Gravity. He loved playing some of Mayer's songs—the bluesy songs were almost meditative for him. But there were only so many of his songs he could play. Nikolaj didn't have short fingers by any means, but Mayer's fingers were so much longer and rehearsed, Nikolaj didn't stand much of a chance.

Nikolaj could sit there playing the same eight or so bars over and over. He then felt more in an acoustic mood, reluctantly put down his electric, and grabbed his birds-eye maple Gibson Epiphone. Like an old friend, he'd had it for over twenty years and knew it well. He started playing James Arthur's Say You Won't Go. He had finally mastered it after a couple of weeks struggle. For whatever reason, he found it difficult to sing it and play the guitar at the same time. Now he just needed to master the chorus which was slightly beyond his vocal comfort level.

After enjoying a few more songs, Kendra headed into the bedroom, brushed her teeth, got into her pajamas, and climbed under the covers. Kendra cracked the window a bit to let in the cool fall air. It was a time to enjoy her surroundings and not worry about the energy bill for a night. Nikolaj came in a little while later after getting ready for bed, turned on the light on his night stand and picked up the latest novel he was working through—the Count of Monte Cristo. After Kendra and her team did the Count of Monte Cristo themed escape room, he decided he should actually read it. It had been on his list for years.

Kendra lay next to him staring up at the ceiling and breathing in the fresh air. She had that feeling of peace and calm that you only get after hard work or a struggle. The kind of feeling you get only occasionally. The feeling that it was all worth it, and that you would do it again—knowing that you *will* do it again, and that it's worth the effort.

She pushed her thoughts away and focused on her breathing and the cool, crisp air coming in from outside. With one last satisfied sigh, she fell to her dreams.

The End

www.ingramcontent.com/pod-product-compliance
Lightning Source LLC
Chambersburg PA
CBHW060146130626
46556CB00006B/2521